DECEPTION ROAD

An Ensley Markus Mystery, Book 2

PEGGY STAGGS

Spinone Press LLC

Spinone Press, LLC

Eagle, Idaho 83616

Visit our website at www.peggystaggs.com

Copyright © 2016 Peggy Staggs

ISBN# 978-0-9968951-2-5

To my friends who've been there through a lot more thin than thick. To the women who keep me on course, Elizabeth Fredericksen and Judy Keim. I couldn't do it without you!

Acknowledgments

A special thanks to Dr. Peggy Rupp, MD. She keeps my arthritic joints in great shape and my characters properly injured.

Chapter One

I knew if I opened the door any hope of a quiet Christmas would vanish. I glared at the man on the other side of the leaded glass window. My former fiancé, Don March was supposed to be in Washington D.C., not Spirit Springs, Idaho. He was *supposed* to be out of my life. Not ringing my doorbell two days before Christmas.

When he saw me, he pushed open the door.

If I'd known he was in town, I would have locked my doors.

I stood my ground. "Don, what are you doing here?"

He didn't say a word, he pushed me back past the entry table, grabbed me, and kissed me. I jerked away and kneed him. My intention was to strike hard enough that his father would feel it. He sunk to the floor. I've been working out. And, yeah, I fight dirty. I figured it was warranted since he had eight inches and a good hundred plus pounds on me. So there Mr. Two-timing-POS.

"Ensley," he gasped.

"That will teach you not to touch people without permission." Jack stood a few inches behind me. He is so quiet even his truck whispers when it's running. Pushing the door closed, he watched Don struggle to get to his feet.

He didn't make it.

1

This Christmas had promised to be difficult. Don's presence squared that difficult quotient. As if that were even possible. I was still trying to gather the fragments of my destroyed career and dealing with my dad dying in my arms. All with nominal success.

"March, what the hell are you doing here?" Jack is used to being in charge, he's Sheriff Jack Trace, of Spirit Springs and more. What, I'm not sure. But I'm working on it.

"Trace," Don grimaced as he worked to get to his feet. "I might... ask you... the same thing."

Oh, please, Don knew exactly why Jack was here. He's the reason I'm wearing a Christmas red cashmere sweater and black silk slacks, and why I'd spent the last hour trying to get my makeup perfect and strong-arming my brown hair into behaving.

Jack is welcome any time he wants to come over.

Don is not.

This time Don's struggle was successful. Now that he was on his feet, I thought an instant replay of my greeting was in order. After all, he had more than a little to do with ending my career. That brought up the memory of him cheating on me with my former supervisor.

I swear at times Jack can read my mind. He put his arm around my shoulders in a kind of you-probably-shouldn't motion. He set a bottle of my favorite wine on the entry table and turned his attention to our intruder. "I was invited," was all he said.

The two men faced each other. Jack's hands curled into fists. Don's did the same.

The last thing I needed right now was a lot of broken furniture. Besides, Jack had just returned from one of his unexplained absences two days ago. He always comes home a little worse for wear. I stepped between them before any punches were thrown.

Both men's cell phones rang.

"Trace."

"March."

They have a shared past, one Jack refuses to talk about. I'm not asking Don. I don't want to speak to him. Ever.

Jack and Don glared at each other as they listened to the voices on the other end of their phones.

Jack glanced at me.

It's a toss-up who knows better what a total bastard Don is. Jack, because he'd had professional dealings with him. Or me, because I'd been semi-engaged to him when he'd cheated on me. I say semi because I had the ring, and I'd told him, no, but he insisted I think about it. Jack and I had both learned the hard way, that the price of contact with Don was always too high.

Both men hung up.

"Doc, there's a situation," Jack said. "I'm sorry. I have to go to the office."

"I've been called to the Sheriff's Office, also." Don forced the words through his clenched jaw as he shot Jack a contemptuous glance.

Jack opened the door and stepped aside. "March." He motioned for Don to leave.

Under the porte-cochere gracing my hundred-year-old-brick home sat Jack's brand-new silver Ford F250. With the snow tires he'd put on it, the vehicle looked ready for anything. His old Ford had met its maker on a mountain road south of town a few days before Halloween. That same day Jack had been shot and we'd nearly been blown up by some ruthless people who were now either awaiting trial or dead.

Don walked out to his car.

I stopped Jack. "I don't want him here."

"I know, neither do I." Jack smiled, then leaned closer and whispered, "I'll be back." His words sent a shiver of expectation through me as I watched him walk away.

Jack is gorgeous, and just, all around great. He's tall, 6'3," with slightly unruly light brown hair. I'm not sure if it's naturally disobedient or if it's more a matter of wear and tear. His hazel eyes captivate me with their kaleidoscope of gold, brown, and green. He has shoulders to die for, and his kisses are a study in seduction. After a couple, my brain is unable to string together a coherent thought as it hungers for the next kiss. Jack is so easy to be with. The thought always makes me smile.

Jack helped me catch the garbage who'd murdered my dad. It was more of a him-solving-it and me-getting-in-the-way situation. Being a doctor — albeit a research physician — had come in handy throughout the process.

Don, on the other hand, is Jack's height. He has striking ice blue eyes and black hair that's expertly cut to lay exactly right. His body is one of someone whose trainer knows precisely what he's doing.

As I stood in the doorway, half of me ached with curiosity to know what circumstances would call these two titans to Jack's office. The other half was happy to let it play out without me.

My only Christmas decoration hung on the front door. A wreath, of pine boughs, had a bright red ribbon twining through the greenery. The frosted pinecones provided the perfect accent. It lay gracefully against my white door. Two weeks ago, Jack and I visited the tree lot in Mullen. We needed three wreaths, one for my place, one for his, and one for the B&B. We'd laughed as we selected the wreaths and two trees. He'd been intent on picking the homeliest tree on the lot. On purpose.

If this had been any other time, I would have smiled at the memory. But with Don showing up I knew I wasn't in any mood to smile.

I watched Don's rental car, followed by Jack's Ford, pull around the driveway and onto the street. Snow began to lightly fall as I leaned on the doorframe. The large flakes against the evergreens reminded me of a Christmas card.

I closed the door and went to change into jeans. Five minutes later, I left Brique House for the B&B. I walked through the grove of pines and leafless deciduous trees veiling my home from the rest of the world. Leaving the darkness of the glen, I came out into a swirl of blowing snow. I glanced up. The clouds had been gathering all day. There'd be no stars tonight, only snow. I pulled my jacket up around my ears.

I wanted to talk to Jane. She'd stayed after my dad died because in her words, "I don't have anywhere else to be, and someone has to see to those cats that just showed up one day." I knew she could go anywhere, and the cats lived with me, sort of. Right now, they were at the B&B, probably guarding one of the heat vents. Since the weather had turned cold, the two of them were constantly in search of a warm spot.

As I came around the corner, I saw the Shaw's car still parked next to the old school building turned B&B.

When the Shaw's checked in three days ago, Jane and I made it clear we'd be closing the twenty-third. Since that was today, I was surprised to see they were still here.

I distracted myself with thoughts of them. They're an odd couple who border on strange. Barbara Shaw is a perfect medium. Her hair is ordinary brown, and her eyes a lifeless tan. She's neither attractive nor unattractive merely average. it was almost as if her goal was to be a perfect average. Her husband Nate is tall, skinny, with shiny black hair, and watery blue eyes. He tracks people with a squinty intensity as if he's studying them. I don't like being the subject of scrutiny.

They'd told us they were here to celebrate a recent large business deal. Yet, they didn't spend much time together. I shrugged. Everyone's relationship is different.

When I'd been with Don, we'd gone to official gatherings or parties and newsworthy events. It had all been very public. Nothing personal. Like a picnic, or a Saturday morning at a farmer's market or even a movie. We'd gone to a few plays, but only if the right people were there. Hindsight is so clear.

Jack is the opposite, we're always doing something special together. Running... well, until winter set in, that's when we began taking walks in the country. The snow floats down around us like a veil of soft lace. Lois, Jack's Spinone loves the white stuff. It provides her with an endless source of fun. We laugh as she sticks her head in a drift. When she pulls out she shakes her long ears, sending snow flying in all directions.

Jack and I even grocery shopped together. I smiled. Nothing is special unless you're with the right person. Jack is my right person. The thought stopped me. I hadn't known him long enough to feel that way. Had I? Be careful.

"Jane," I called as I walked in the back door.

"In here, Boss." I found her in the dining room half of her sticking out from under the Christmas tree. She was reaching for something at the base of it. She came up with Mason, our big black-and-white cat and resident scoundrel. He delights in disassembling what he can and knocking the rest to the floor. Cats.

Jane let him go, and he scampered up onto a nearby chair. The boughs of the tree had restyled Jane's soft blonde hair. "That cat is a rascal." She pulled her sweatshirt down around her slim waste.

Around us, the dining room was decorated with red and green plaid tablecloths. The pine centerpieces with their bright colored candles gave the room a festive atmosphere.

Neither decorations nor the sparkling lights on the tree could restore my good spirits. "Let me help," I said. We returned the silver garland to its rightful place on the tree. I reached out, saving a red ornament from smashing on the vintage hardwood floors.

"Thanks. That crazy cat is set on taking this tree down one decoration at a time." The cats arrived at the B&B a month before I did. Someone had thrown them away like last week's garbage. Fortunately, they landed in Jane's backyard.

Mason rolled on his back and stretched his paws out as if to say, "Come play with me." When no one obliged him, he sat up and began taking a kitty bath.

Mattie, the gray tabby, lay in a sunny spot on the sill of one of the tall windows gracing the front of the building. I went to where she lay. This window overlooked the snowy meadow out front. Even with all the white, the memories of that dark October night flooded back. I could still see the life-light fade from my dad's eyes as I held him in my arms. It was a memory that would live with me forever.

"I thought the Shaws were checking out today," I said as I turned from the window.

"They asked if they could stay until later this evening. I didn't see any harm." She paused. "Ah. We aren't guest-free."

No.

Please, don't let it be Don. I needed him to be passing through. Anything, *anything*, except what I knew she was going to say. "Oh?" I held on to my glass half-full attitude.

"A man came by earlier, said he was a friend of yours and Jack's and needed a room for a while."

"Was he tall, dark hair, blue eyes, attractive?"

She nodded. "He said his name was Don March."

My glass not only spilled, it shattered.

She studied me. "He's not a friend?"

"No. He's the man I was engaged to in D.C. It'll be okay." I knew it wouldn't.

"I thought about sayin' no. The name sounded familiar, but I couldn't place it." She tilted her head. "He said you were expecting him."

Of course, he did. He'd say, or do anything to get what he wanted. The problem was I had no idea what his plans were.

"I remember now, he's the one who got you fired." She stood straight and put her hands on her hips. "I'll throw him out."

I smiled. "Let's hope he finishes what he came here to do, and leaves." Nothing was ever easy with Don.

"He does seem like the determined sort." She picked up the big cat to keep him from rearranging the garland again. "He knows we're closed Christmas Eve and Day. No breakfast. He said he had plans."

I could only imagine what they were. It didn't matter. Uncle Stan was coming, and we were all going to Jack's tomorrow. I couldn't wait. The magic of Christmas has always held the promise of a new beginning for me. I know most people consider New Year's Day as the beginning. It's always been Christmas for me. I sighed as my phone vibrated in my pocket. Jack's picture appeared on the screen. "Hi, Jack."

"Meet me at the bar and grill." He hung up. The tightness in his voice was in stark contrast to his whispered words earlier. He hadn't said goodbye. He always said goodbye.

Judging by his tone, nothing good had happened at his office. I handed Jane a Christmas card. "I've got to go. I was going to mail this, but since they're still here, would you give it to the Shaws? There's a coupon inside for next year. Please, wish them a Merry Christmas for us."

She took the envelope. "Is this Don March going to cause us trouble?" Jane and I had been through a lot in our short time together. Dad's death had hit us both hard. Jack and I nearly getting killed a few days later hadn't made things any easier. I was ready for a quiet, uneventful holiday.

"Oh, without a doubt."

She sighed. "We don't need any more excitement." With a glance at the envelope in her hand, she said, "I'll take the cats to your place."

"Thanks. I'll see you later." Brique House is a large two-story brick structure. Hence the name. I wondered why they'd used the French spelling. I'd asked Jane if she'd wanted to share the large house with me. She'd said no. She liked her little place near the old stables. I'm sure it has more to do with Uncle Stan's visits than the house. They have an arrangement.

I hurried and slipped back into my silk slacks and red sweater. They'd be cold, but they'd look great. I'd abandoned my Christian Louboutin's as outdoor wear for the season. Two feet of snow, plus four-inch heels, equals something broken. I took them with me. It doesn't snow inside.

I walked up to the Hot Springs Bar and Grill ten minutes later. The only dinner restaurant in town is a large log structure. Outside Christmas lights outlined the eaves. Above the main entrance hung a six-foot wreath.

In the coat room, I put on my black heels. Hey, you can take the girl out of the city, but you can't take away her shoes. I hung my jacket and shoe bag on one of the hooks.

Inside it was body to body. Holiday music intertwined with the laughter and conversation of the patrons. The massive elk antlers above the equally impressive stone fireplace were festooned with tiny blinking lights. The poor animal was probably rolling over in his grave.

As I scanned the room for Jack, Lacey Harris stepped in front of me. She's the bartender here and the mayor's daughter. Her long nails dug into my arm. A cluster of mistletoe clung to her long, straight red hair. At least, it was red this week. "Jack wasn't enough for you?"

"What?" She is under the illusion I stole Jack from her. Their relationship is a figment of her imagination.

"Don was here earlier today asking all about you. He's back, and he wants to see you as soon as you get here." She squeezed my arm tighter. "Are you going to leave with Don? Why wouldn't you? You and your fancy clothes don't belong here. He's gorgeous and big city. Maybe I'll have a go at him. Yeah, I'd like all those fancy people back east."

Poor Lacey. "Don isn't the kind of man —"

"Are you kidding? He's handsome and important. He isn't like the cowboys around here." She hesitated as if to put extra emphasis on her next words. "Or a small-town sheriff." She shook my arm hard.

Don has a ruthless James Bond façade. "Lacey, you —" I started over. "I'm not going anywhere." I decided to ignore the reference to Jack. It wouldn't do any good to go down that road again. I pried her vice-like fingers loose.

She grasped my arm back. "What do you do for these guys?"

Don's arrival had ruined my evening with Jack, and now Lacey was in the process of making my bad mood, worse. "Why don't *you* leave with Don?" I thought it was worth a shot. Maybe she'd be happy with the D.C., life.

"I could if I wanted. But I'm not giving up on Jack. He'll get tired of you and come back to me."

"Where are they?" The conversation had gone full circle and I was tired of her ridiculous rantings.

"At the back table." She spun around and returned to the bar.

Leaving me to wonder if it was snowing in her world, too.

I zigzagged my way through the jovial crowd toward the back table. It's tucked in a corner where the light bulb mysteriously always needs to be replaced. Lovers use the faint glow seclusion to their advantage.

Jack and Don were intent as they faced each other across the small table. As I drew closer, I heard them talking.

"I'll tell her everything, Trace. Then we'll see what she thinks of you. See how long she stays," Don said as he leaned forward.

The look on Jack's face stopped me. His eyes were hard, and I knew he was struggling to control his anger. "She won't believe you," he said.

"Maybe not, but it'll plant a seed of doubt. She'll start questioning what kind of monster you really are." Don leaned back in his chair. "She questions everything. She'll start to dig and —"

Jack glanced up. He stood. "Doc." He smiled and pulled a chair out for me.

Don stood.

It struck me how much the two men were built alike. Tall and muscular. If the lights were any lower, I wouldn't be able to tell them apart.

"Thank you." I sat next to Jack.

Lacey sauntered over, her eyes locked on Don. "Can I refresh your drink?" The yarn in her bright green sweater strained against her ample chest.

"Please." He smiled at her. The same practiced smile he'd trained on me a hundred times.

When she left, I asked, "Why are we here?" More precisely, why was *I* here?

"We're waiting," Don said.

I was about to ask the question again when Lacey returned. "That guy." She turned to point to someone. She had a confused look on her face as she turned back to us. "He was there a second ago." She shrugged. "Anyway, he wanted me to give this to you." She held out an envelope.

Jack reached for it, and she snatched it back. "It's for Don." Lacey touched Don's hand as she presented it to him. With an enticing grin, she ran her long red fingernail up his arm and rested her hand on his shoulder.

I thought she was going to hold out for Jack? Now it seemed Don was in her sights. Or was she trying to make Jack jealous? Poor Lacey. She shot Jack a glance to be sure he was watching. He wasn't.

"Thank you." Don gave her another smile and squeezed her hand. When we were alone, he ripped open the envelope, then showed it to us.

"It's empty," I said. I still had no idea why I was here.

"It's a go," Jack said.

As Don took out cash, Jack whispered, "I'll drive you home."

He knew as well as I did, I had my car. I'd pick it up later.

As we made our way through the crowd I asked again, "Jack, why am I here?"

"He ordered me to call you. I don't want you involved in this... situation." He paused. "None of this feels right."

Was Don, Jack's boss? That had to be a toxic combination.

As we walked through the happy crowd, Jack shifted gears and said, "I'm impressed." We wove through the patrons. "How'd you get in here, without falling, in those shoes, with all this snow? Or is it one of your girl secrets?"

When I'd first arrived in Spirit Springs, I'd had a problem navigating the town's crumbling sidewalks. "Trade secret." I slid my hand into his. Touching him always made me feel like I was seventeen, experiencing the thrill of being with my first real boyfriend. Jack is no boy.

He stopped and faced me. "This isn't what I'd planned for tonight."

I could tell by the way he'd said he'd be back. "What's going on?" I asked.

"I can't tell you. It's classified which makes your presence completely out of line."

Classified? Interesting. "So why *am* I here?"

Jack scanned the crowd. For a second his attention settled on Don as he talked to someone at the bar. "Not here." I felt the muscles in his arm tighten.

I got my bag and jacket from the coat room. He pushed the door open, and we walked out into a wall of large snowflakes. I held fast to his arm.

"I want you safe. I don't know what he's trying to accomplish, but for tonight he's calling the shots. This is" — he stopped — "an unusual circumstance."

Jack told me once Don had saved his life. He'd also said the debt was paid. "I don't want anything to do with him." Then it occurred to me — "Don, isn't your boss, is he?"

"God, no. This whole thing has a —" He struggled with what to say as we stopped beside his truck. He brushed a flake from my face. "I want this over and him gone." He kissed me.

Jack knows his kisses distract me because I've told him so. From the smile on his face when I told him... let's just say he is more than happy to divert my attention, and I'm eager to let him. "You're asserting your unfair advantage."

"If I had a choice —" He shook his head as he opened the truck door for me.

The five-minute ride to my house was silent. I wasn't sure if Jack was concentrating on the snow-slick road or the upcoming mission. I sat next to him wishing I had the power to send Don back to Washington or better Mars. It would be the best Christmas present ever. I wasn't going to let this go. I wanted answers.

We stopped under the porte-cochere, and I put my hand on his arm. "Tell me what's going on." Don's words still echoed through my mind. "I'm telling her everything."

Jack pressed his lips together. "It's classified." He isn't only the sheriff, he's ex-Delta Force. Every now and then he vanishes for a few days. So, I'm not sure if he's ex or not. I've often wondered where people think he goes on those sudden trips. I asked Phyllis once, she'd expertly dodged the question.

Jack helped me out of the truck. He wrapped me in his arms and his warm citrus aftershave filled my senses.

"Come in," I whispered. "I'll make a fire."

He kissed me again. "Tomorrow night." He hesitated as if to say something more. Instead, he kissed me one more time then got back in his truck.

I watched as he pulled out onto the street and vanished behind a wall of snow.

Tomorrow night. The words echoed in my head.

Chapter Two

I climbed the stairs to my bedroom. I kicked off my shoes and left them where they landed. I always put my shoes away. Tonight, I didn't care.

One of my coping mechanisms is list making. I find they help me focus on the problem facing me and checking things off gives me a feeling of accomplishment. Since I had no idea what was going on, I wouldn't be checking things off this list. No, wait. I could write Don's name a hundred times, then invent different ways to obliterate it. Okay, that would only work if I was fourteen. I sat on my bed, I had to fit the pieces together.

At the top of the sheet I wrote:

Things I don't like. This could take two pages.

Don being here. I underlined it three times.

The way things were headed. Well, no kidding.

The conversation I'd overheard in the bar. A couple more underlines.

Jack going along with it. Whatever it was. Underline, exclamation point. It was a good thing I was using a pen, I would have broken a pencil in half by now.

The fact it happened the night before Christmas Eve.

Why was Don here? I knew why he'd kissed me. He's an ass and the feels like he can… should… and does own me. I'd given him back his engagement ring right before I'd showed him the picture of him and his *other woman*. I'd explained — as calmly as I could — how I found his behavior unacceptable. I'd told him I never wanted to see him, ever. Twice. Once in person, and once on the phone after my dad's death. I'd deleted his number from my phone. Okay, the last one hadn't affected him at all. It had made me feel better.

I asked myself, why Jack? Don has lots of men under him. CIA Agents. And by the way, what was *this* thing he was having Jack do? I added those to the list, too.

I laid down. The puffy floral comforter rose to welcome me. The cats were already snuggled in . Sometimes, I think it belongs to them, and they let me share it.

I still marveled at this feeling of being home, of the belonging. At first, I thought it was because Spirit Springs was where my dad had settled. That wasn't it. I'd been here several times to visit. I'd stayed in this very room. I'd picked out the duvet and curtains. The books on the shelves were mine.

It had to be the people. Jack made me happy. I couldn't help the smile I felt on my lips. He'd included me in his life. I even kept his dog, Lois, when he left town. I felt important to him. I glanced at the chandelier above.

The problem came with my lousy track record with men. My nearly yearlong relationship with Don was front and center. He'd seemed like a good guy in the beginning, too. Jack was different… he had to be. He just had to be.

As a military kid, I'd moved, it seemed like every year. Transferring from one duty station to the next taught me one thing above all, *nothing is permanent*. I'd never experienced this sensation of being home anywhere else. This place, these people… I felt too comfortable, too happy. I even had cats now. I glanced over at Mason, the big male stopped snoring as he rolled over on his back.

Jane had become a great friend. Uncle Stan's visits completed our happy makeshift family. The one thing missing was my former assistant, Sophie and her family. They'd welcomed me into their number the first time I'd met them.

Family. A blast of anxiety rattled through me. Too much, too soon. I had to slow down, give things a chance to play out in real time, not let this rush of emotions overwhelm me. I shivered. Jack hadn't pressured me for anything more than the pleasure of his company and his kisses. He was and wasn't the problem. It was everything coming at me too fast. I've always heard relationships based on intense situations never work. I started another list.

How long would it be before time robbed me of this place and these people, these loved ones?

Neither the ceiling nor the delicate crystal chandelier hanging from it were giving me any answers. I needed to talk to Jack. I know it sounds crazy since he was the main reason I needed to apply the brakes. But there it was. I tell him things I don't tell anyone else. Not even my best friend Sophie. Fear spread through me... again. If things ended badly this time, I wasn't sure there'd be a road back for me.

I rolled over and looked at the clock. It was nearly midnight. Jack was probably asleep. The only thing I'd been able to get out of him earlier was *it* began in the morning.

Perfect. Christmas Eve.

Instead of being considerate, I called Jack.

"Hi," he answered.

"I don't like this thing Don has you doing. I don't want you hurt again. I know you're healed from the bullet wound in October, but tomorrow... today is Christmas Eve, and you're going off to do who knows what. You can't, Uncle Stan will be here —" I was pretty sure I'd just slipped off the sanity rail — "and I don't want any more turmoil, and I want Don gone. I don't want you involved in anything that has to do with him. I don't trust him."

"Neither do I, this is a simple exchange, I'll be back before dinner."

I heard a noise on his end of the phone.

"I'll call you right back."

"No, wait." Too late.

I shouldn't have called. Jack needed rest for this *simple* thing tomorrow. If Don was involved it was a sure bet, nothing would be easy about it.

I got up and walked to the window. In the glow of the porch light below, I could see the snow as it sauntered down to meet what had already fallen. It was as if the flakes were unsure if they wanted to call this town home.

All the experts tell you not to make any major decisions for a year after a traumatic event. I wondered if I should count each situation individually, or lump them all together. I lumped them. I didn't want to put the next seven or eight years of my life on hold. I hoped tonight wouldn't add to my total.

I took a deep breath, and said to the cats, "I need a reliable stress relief system. Maybe a combination of running, yoga and meditation. I can't run in the snow. Maybe I should get a treadmill. No, I hate those things."

Jack brought a whole different dimension to my anxiety level. We'd met the first night I was in town. He'd pulled a gun on me, but the situation was desperate. He thought I'd shot my dad. It was a reasonable assumption since he lay dead on the ground behind me. In full discloser, I'd pointed my gun at him first.

I held up my cell phone. Twenty minutes had passed.

The half-full glass of optimism in my head was bone dry. Uncle Stan would be here tomorrow. I glanced at the clock, no tonight. His arrival would make Jane happy. Me, too. Even though he wasn't my real uncle, I loved him as if he were.

The plan was to spend Christmas Eve together at Jack's. I wouldn't be making a drunken pass at him tonight. Too much wine, too much chaos, and no self-control had led to an unforced error on my part in October. I didn't need the wine now. I couldn't help but smile. I was content with his kisses and to hold him. For now.

"Slow down," I said out loud. I sighed and let my gaze wander around my room. The gifts I still needed to wrap were lined up on the window seat. One of the toys I'd gotten Lois had fallen to the floor. No doubt, Mason's handy work. "Crazy cat."

After replacing it, I went downstairs for a drink of water. As I passed through the entry, I thought I saw a wisp of light and shadow sweep through the library.

I shivered. Jane's nephew had died about where I was standing, murdered by the man intent on killing me. "Probably one of the resident ghosts I keep hearing about." The scientist part of my brain rationalized it was more likely the reflections of headlights from the main road filtering through the trees.

I smiled. Ghosts. Jane's Nana was going to clear the house of spirits on New Year's Day. Nana — everyone just calls her Nana — assured me it was the best time. I wondered how she was going to banish the spirits. Jane said it wouldn't hurt after all the deaths in the house. I was sure it wasn't necessary. I figured our spirits have better things to do after we die than hang around righting perceived wrongs or scaring the bejesus out of the living. Still, I liked Nana, there was something mysterious about her.

I hoped the banishment didn't involve hanging garlic in the windows. No, that was for vampires. A séance would be interesting. Maybe not. When they have them in old movies, it leads to more ghosts, and inevitably someone dying. My thoughts had come full circle. Damn it. I didn't want any more dead anyone or anything.

I rubbed my bare arms. I'd bought this negligee for Don. Not only why was I wearing it? Then there was the question; why did I still have it? The still-having-it part was most likely because it cost two-hundred dollars. It was going in the trash right now.

I tossed the pink lace garment in the trash. "On second thought." I retrieved it. It's pretty. I'd donate it. Someone else will like it. I put on different nightwear.

Thirty minutes had passed. He'd call, I thought as I went in and brushed my teeth, again.

I left the bathroom and informed the cats, "He's had long enough." I picked up my phone and hit Jack's contact.

No answer. "He must be busy. Had Don moved up the mission?"

No. Jack would have called.

I waited.

At one a.m. I decided something was wrong, and got dressed. On the stairs, I stopped before I reached the entry. "This is absolute insanity. He'll call."

I knew I wouldn't sleep if I didn't do something. "Shit. This man is so much trouble." I'm not much of a wait-and-see person. Besides, I couldn't deny the apprehension that was swarming around me like a mass of mosquitoes. I don't have ESP, it comes down to Jack being a man of his word. There was a valid reason he hadn't called. I knew I should wait, but again — not great at waiting.

Jack had brought me home, so I didn't have a car. It would take me fifteen minutes or more in this snow to walk back to the bar and grill. I'd borrow Jane's truck. I hurried to the house behind the old stables.

I knocked.

A light came through an upstairs window. A minute later, the porch light blinked on clear and bright. As soon as the door opened, I started talking. "Jane, I need to borrow your truck. Jack's not answering his phone."

"He's probably asleep like a person should be." She yawned.

"No. I was talking to him. That was over an hour ago, he said he'd call me right back. Now he isn't answering his phone."

"I'll get dressed."

"No. I just need to use your truck."

"Keys are in it."

I ran for the truck.

"Call me. I'll worry," Jane shouted through the falling snow. Two inches now covered the truck, and it was coming down harder.

Starting Jane's oxidized red heap is hit-and-miss on a warm day. It's older than I am. I'm not sure it isn't older than she is. I prayed it would start. To sweeten the deal, I promised it new seat covers if it started. To my surprise, the bribe worked. I drove past the B&B. Don's rental car sat near the front of the building. I couldn't blame him this time.

»§«

A burst of sanity hit me as I pulled to a stop in front of Jack's. This was crazy. Anything might be keeping him from calling. I backed up. "I should go home and–

I slammed on the brakes, killed the engine and jumped out.

Jack's front door stood open. The Christmas wreath gone.

In Idaho, in the mountains, in December, you don't leave your door open. I grab my .38 from my purse.

I took the front steps two at a time and ran for the front door.

Maybe he was outside. I stepped through the door onto the sandstone entry. If he had been out here, he'd be back by now if he was able. "Jack?" I whispered his name into the black cold night. "Where are you?"

Nothing.

Only the gentle sound of snow falling on snow.

I reached inside the front door and flipped on the lights.

His elegant living room lay in shambles. Furniture tipped over, lamps broken and the Christmas tree lay on the floor. Blood marred one of the cream-colored couches. I took a panic-releasing breath and stomped my fear into submission. I'm good in desperate times. This was definitely one of those times.

I heard a bark come from deep in the house. "Lois?"

My gun raised, I went to the bottom of the stairs leading to the bedrooms. "Jack," I called.

I took each step with slow deliberation. If something was wrong, which it was, I'd deal with it. "He's probably outside, and he'll be right back." The words sounded even more stupid out loud than they had in my head.

Another bark. Lois would never leave Jack.

A body lay sprawled in the middle of the spacious hall. Thank God, it wasn't Jack. The blood stains on the man's shirt were directly over his heart. I checked for signs of life, anyway. He was dead.

"Jack." My heart pounded as an adrenalin surge heightened my senses.

Lois's bark came from Jack's room.

I wiped the sweat from my upper lip on my shoulder as I reached for the doorknob. I knew I should stop and call for help, but what if Lois was hurt. Or worse, Jack.

Logic struggled past my physical symptoms. Jack wasn't inside. The dead guy was in the hall. I pushed the door open. The bedside table lay on the floor. Next, to it, the broken was still lit. Lois came to me, head down, tail wagging. I knelt and hugged her to me.

Jack's beautiful room was trashed. The pictures of his Army buddies hung at dangerous angles. One had a bullet hole in it. Blood trailed down the doorjamb beside me.

Was it Jack's or the dead man's?

My breathing now came in rapid bursts. "Lois."

I pushed her back and checked her for injuries. She wasn't hurt, but she was as scared as I was. "Let's find Jack."

We walked into the hall. Written in blood above the body were the words, "We have him."

I froze. Beside me, Lois whined.

I needed help.

Uncle Stan was too far away. I didn't have Jack's FBI friend's number. I wasn't going to blindly call the field office in Salt Lake City and get some stranger who wouldn't care — if anyone was even there this early on Christmas Eve. Jack's deputies didn't have any experience with kidnappings. Only one person in town had the expertise to get things done fast. I hesitated.

This was a mistake.

I knew it.

He was the only one.

I dialed his number, I wasn't even sure he'd help.

He answered on the third ring. "March," his voice was hoarse with sleep.

"Don, it's Ensley —"

"Hi, honey."

I ignored the honey part. "Jack's been kidnapped."

"Where are you?"

"At his house."

"How do you know he's been kidnapped?" He yawned.

"Get over here now. You got him into this, you're going to get him out of it." I hung up one second before I realized I hadn't told him where Jack lived. No, Don would know. He seemed to know everything else. I called back anyway. I was right. He knew.

Ten minutes later, Don pulled up in front of Jack's large brick home. Lois and I were huddled on the steps outside as his headlights panned across us.

"What's going on?" he asked as he got out of his car.

"In here." I showed him the body, the torn-up rooms and the message on the wall. "What did you get him into?"

"He's a big boy, he can take care of himself," the tone of Don's voice was flat and dismissive.

Don was the last person in the entire world I would have voluntarily gone to. The last person I trusted to do the right thing.

There was no one else.

I faced him. "This is how it's going to be. You *are* going to tell me what's going on. You *are* going to find him and bring him back to me, or I swear to God, I'll shoot your ass where you stand." A flash of regret shot through me. Had I just alienated the one person in town who could help me?

I'm not used to confronting people, especially not people like Don. His very presence commands attention. I'd seen it happen time and again. Heads turned when he walked into a room. People would actually step aside.

For a long minute, he searched my face. He's as practiced at keeping his emotions hidden as Jack is. His expressions range from hard to very hard. His coke-bottle blue eyes are ghost-like, vague, and unfeeling.

My adrenaline had ebbed and I knew the man in front of me was my only hope. "Why are you here?"

"You called me." When he didn't want to answer a question, he had a habit of stating the obvious.

I squeezed my eyes shut. "What have you done?"

Chapter Three

"What do you expect me to do?" Don asked.

"You've got connections. Call them."

"I don't have anyone out here." He waved his hand at the darkness.

"Is that the reason you're having Jack do this? No, wait. Kidnapping … FBI … Brad." What was Brad's last name? His number would be in Jack's contacts on his phone.

"Brad Hughes?"

Don wasn't all the help I'd hoped he'd be. I notice he'd taken out his phone.

I dialed Jack's number. Half of me hoped he still had his cell so we'd be able to track him. The other half wanted to find it so I'd be able to call Brad. My heart seized as I heard it ring from inside Jack's bedroom.

I pulled Jack's handmade red, white, and blue quilt from the floor.

On the far side of the room, Don bent down. He reached under the bed and fumbled with something. "Here it is." He hesitated before he stood. Finally, he walked around the bed and handed me the phone.

I pressed the contacts. I glanced down the list of what should have been names. "This is in code." I'd exchanged the conglomeration of letters and numbers that showed on the screen when Jack called for his picture.

Don didn't hear me. He'd moved to the window as he talked on his phone. He raised his voice. "I said I want your men up here now. I know this place is hell and gone from civilization. I'm aware it's one-thirty on Christmas Eve morning. Don't give me excuses. Do it!" He hung up.

I'd never seen the CIA agent side of him. Good, I needed him to be competent.

He walked around the room grabbing blankets and throwing them aside, righting furniture. Finally, he stomped into the closet.

I'd never been in Jack's closet — why would I? "What're you looking for?" I asked from the doorway.

"The exchange money." He began opening drawers. "This mission is falling apart."

And... I was wrong. It was all about his goal. "What about Jack?"

He didn't answer, he just kept going through Jack's things.

I opted not to tell Don he was a jerk. Instead, I moved from one section of the closet to the next. A row of garment bags hung in one section, dress shirts and slacks in another, and jeans and t-shirts in a third. What held my attention was how each area — save the garment bags — transitioned from neat and orderly — almost alphabetically — into normal disarray. As if at one time he'd had nothing better to do than file them.

I touched the t-shirt Jack had worn the day we'd gone wreath shopping. It hung off-center. I felt the soft fabric, knowing what had changed in his life. Me.

"Ensley," Don's voice sounded harsh.

I couldn't pull my eyes from the shirt. I was lost in the idea that I was this important to him. Was I right? I hoped so.

"Ensley."

I drew my attention away from the t-shirt. "What?"

Instead of answering me, he turned me away from the clothes. "Listen to me, the money isn't here. The mission can't go forward without it." He walked out of the closet.

The last thing on my mind was *the mission*. "What about Jack?" I called as I followed him.

The hard expression he'd focused on Jack earlier, he now aimed at me.

"You planned this. How could you, son-of-a-bitch?" I wanted to rip his heart out and show it to him.

"I can see Trace has had an unfortunate effect on your vocabulary and your composure."

I'd show him composure. I stepped up to him. Over his shoulder, I could see the bloody words scrawled on the wall and feel Jack's dog by my side. "If you had anything to do with this I'll kill you myself." My hand balled into a fist.

He gazed down at me and shook his head. "He isn't worth it. Of course, he hasn't told you how he can afford this house. Or why he's hiding in this backwater town in the middle of a backwater state, has he?" He paused. "He ruined his life, your father's and Stan Hofstadter's. Now, how does your hero sound?"

"I've seen you do this time and again. It won't work on me." More times than I could count, he'd level a man with a half-truth or an innuendo. I wouldn't let it happen this time. "I know his grandmother left him all her money. Interesting how things have changed. Jack talks to me. He even asks my advice. Besides, why wouldn't you live where you want to?" Okay, the advice part had been about some pillows his decorator wanted him to buy. But, hey, he'd asked. Don had never asked my opinion on anything. By the way, Jack got the pillows I liked.

I stood in silence watching Don walk away. "Are you coming?" he called as he left the room. "I'm not jeopardizing my career for Trace."

I rubbed Lois's ears. "I'll find him," I whispered. I prayed he'd be alive when I did.

One thing for sure, Don will do anything to save himself, even if it means saving Jack.

»§«

I hurried to catch Don as he got in his car. I opened the back door for Lois.

"I don't want a dog in here."

"Too bad." I slammed the passenger's door as I got in.

"Fine. I don't care. It's a rental." The headlights panned across Jane's truck. "Where did you get the wreck?"

"It's a friend's."

"Nice." He backed up.

"What have you gotten Jack into?" I stuffed my gun in my jacket pocket. "And don't tell me it's a simple exchange. That ship has dropped anchor in a foreign port." I indicated Jack's house and what had happened there.

"All he had to do was take the money to my informant and bring back the information."

"Nothing is that easy with you. Who's the informant?"

"Damion La Clair."

I hated when he used this tactic. Technically, it was an answer, but it didn't tell me anything. "Stop it."

"He's one of my operatives. He infiltrated a terrorist organization. They all crossed the southern border and made their way up to Idaho. He's due here today to hand over vital information on an upcoming —"

"Terrorists." My heart pounded so hard I gasped. "Why would they come to Idaho?"

"The nuclear plant," was all he said.

"Why involve Jack? It doesn't make any sense."

"It does if you know the odds."

I gripped the leather seat. "The odds?" Were they skewed against Jack? The thought sent another adrenaline surge through me. At this rate, my adrenal gland was going to self-destruct. I gripped the leather seat. "Did you send him on a suicide mission?" No, wait — "How can you, he isn't in the Army any longer?"

"It's classified."

Jack had said the same thing. Maybe this would work. "And telling me terrorists are planning something involving the INL near Twin Falls isn't?" Hold on. "If you know the who, then you've got to know the where."

He shook his head. "No. This is too important to interfere with. I shouldn't have told you this much."

I seized him by his collar. The element of surprise worked in my favor... sort of. The car swerved on the slick road, but Don quickly forced it back to a straight path. Okay, I didn't think my actions all the way through. He was driving, the road was solid snow and ice, and it was the middle of the night. On the plus side, I now had his full attention. I let him go.

He braked. "Control yourself."

He was right. This wouldn't help find Jack. The panic I felt doubled. Now, I not only had to find Jack, but I also had to stop the terrorists from blowing up a good portion of Idaho, Nevada, and Utah. Terrorists. It made sense. No one else would have the expertise to take him. "I'm sorry. You don't understand." The only thing I could think about was Jack at the hands of radicals.

"Oh, I think I do." He put the car in park and angled toward me. "He was here when your father died. He played the big hero didn't he?" Don leaned against the door and crossed his arms as he leveled his gaze on me. "Stop me if I get anything wrong. He did everything to solve the case. He included you in the investigation. Told you how much your father meant to him. Even said he owed him. Eventually, he found the killers and saved the day. Everyone's hero. Did I miss anything? When all was settled, he claimed his prize. You. I've seen him do it dozens of times, honey, and you fell for it." He leaned forward and put out his hand to caress my cheek.

I slapped it away. "Knock it off." I didn't believe a word of it. I'd learned the hard way Don is a consummate liar.

My leather seat groaned as I confronted him. "If he ruined the lives of my dad and Uncle Stan why are they such good friends? Uncle Stan is coming to spend Christmas with us, with Jack." Let's hear the answer, Mr. I-know-everything.

He took hold of the steering wheel. For a long moment, he considered the snow falling on the hood of the car. "Interesting relationship. They all ended up rich, didn't they?"

Don was calling three of the men in my life dishonest, and dishonorable. I wouldn't let it stand. "You're wrong. Dad and Uncle Stan spent their lives serving this country. They sacrificed and earned every dollar they have. I know how much Jack means to Uncle Stan and how close he was to my dad. For God's sake, my dad's last words were to trust Jack. He's as honorable as they are."

"The facts stand." Don put the car in gear and continued down the road.

He'd done it again. *The facts stand.* He knew how much I relied on facts. I wanted to choke the truth out of him. I had to refocus. If I didn't, I ran the risk of losing the help of the only person who could find Jack. Right now, I was more anxious to find him than fight with Don. "Where do we start?"

"We wait for my men to get here."

Hold on. If there were terrorists with plans to blow up the INL, who was going to pull off the exchange? Shouldn't it be Homeland or the FBI? I thought it was worth mentioning. "You can't operate inside the country." Did he needed a reminder?

"Special circumstances. Homeland is on the way."

I stared down at Jack's phone. I'd held it tight since Don handed it to me. It felt like a lifetime ago. I took a deep breath as I ran my finger over the touch screen. I couldn't read Jack's code. I wanted Brad here. I stood fixed in place gaping at an instrument that held all the answers, answers that were hidden in a code I had no hope of deciphering.

"Ensley, we need—"

My glance shot to Don. "If this mission is so important, what're you going to do now, with Jack gone?"

He was silent too long. Then he said, "With this weather, I don't know if the operative can get to the rendezvous point."

He was right. What had started as a cheery holiday snow flurry yesterday morning, was now a full-blown blizzard. The wind had begun to whip through the area, and the snow was coming down heavier by the minute.

Don parked in front of the Sheriff's Office.

"Why are we here?" The lights were out. "They don't staff the office at night. I'll call 911." I knew the person answering would be the only deputy on duty.

"This is Deputy Lyle Purdy, what's your emergency?"

"Lyle, it's Ensley Markus. Jack is missing, and we need to get into the Sheriff's Office."

"What?" I heard him start his truck. Lyle had joined the force two months ago. So, this was the blind calling the slightly less blind.

"There's a CIA agent here, and we need to get into the office."

"I'll call Phyllis." He hung up.

"I'm a senior director," Don corrected me.

Don had developed the unique ability to set my nerves on edge with just a word or two. No, it wasn't him it was me. Now, I saw him for what he was. What was setting me off was the idea I hadn't seen it before. I needed to calm down. I couldn't concentrate on finding Jack if my brain was engulfed in Don's half-truths and distractions. Controlling my breathing would help bring my blood pressure closer to normal. Mentally, I held the door closed on the too thin, too nervous woman in my head who oversees apprehension and anxiety. I didn't need her getting loose and jumping off the cliff and into oblivion. That never ended well. I focused on organizing my thoughts as I watched a gust of wind swirl the snow through the night.

I wondered how long it would take Phyllis to arrive. "Why are we here?" I asked for a second time.

"We need a command center."

"So, we *are* going after Jack." I'd begun to doubt he'd be the help I needed.

He turned to me. "I thought that's what you wanted."

"This has been a rough couple of months." I sighed away the memories. "Of course, I want to find him."

"You need to know the real story about Trace." He considered me for a moment. "I don't think this is the time. You're too upset."

My blood pressure spiked. Before I could explain exactly how *upset* I was, a car pulled to a stop in front of us, and Phyllis got out.

Without a word, we left Don's rental. I let Lois out of the backseat.

"Lyle said Jack was missing." Phyllis put her key in the lock.

A grouping of jingle bells hanging on the front door tinkled happily as we entered. Inside, Phyllis shrugged off her coat and turned to me. "Doctor Markus, what's going on?" She set her bag on the desk. "And who are you?" she faced Don.

"CIA." He flipped out his wallet. "Where's Trace's office?"

Phyllis stepped between Don and Jack's office. "You don't have any jurisdiction in my town." She crossed her arms.

"Jack's missing. Kidnapped." The words physically hurt to say.

"Oh, my God. Should I call Oliver?"

"Who's Oliver?" Don asked.

"He's Jack's senior deputy. He's been on the force for six years." Phyllis hadn't given an inch.

I thought calling Oliver was a good idea, at least it would be one more person on Jack's side. "You should call him."

"No. I'm handling this." Don brushed past Phyllis and walked toward Jack's office. "A team will be here by six or seven a.m."

I grasped his arm. "We have to act now. We can't wait four or five hours." I figured he knew that better than I did. So why wasn't he doing what he supposedly did the best? Be a big time CIA Senior Director.

Don glanced down at me.

Before he could say anything, I asked Phyllis, "Where does Jack keep his contacts?"

"On his computer. But it won't do any good," she said. "You need his password. You are not going into my sheriff's office." She moved as if she was going to block Don's path.

Don stepped past me and glared at Phyllis. "I need an office. Trace has the only one." He walked into the room.

I watched Don as I pondered passwords. Most people use dates, names they can remember and believe it or not, the word password. I knew from his phone, Jack's wouldn't be anything easy. I pulled his cell from my pocket. I should have thought of this earlier. Stress and fear were stealing my brain power. I clicked on recent calls, only to find all names encrypted. The numbers weren't. I sat down at one of the empty desks and quickly picked out Uncle Stan's number. No, wait. "Phyllis, do you have Brad Hughes's number in Salt Lake?" She had to have it.

"The FBI agent who was here in October?" she asked. "Let me see." Phyllis pulled out a binder and began leafing through it. "The only number I have is for the field office down there."

I could do this. "What's the area code?"

"There are two. Eight zero one and three eight five. "

I found three calls with those area codes. I pressed the first one. It was two-thirty in the morning on Christmas Eve. I was going to severely annoy someone.

"Who the hell is this? Do you know what time it is?"

"Sir, this is—"

"Whoever you are you've got the wrong number." The line went dead. I took solace in that it wasn't Brad's voice.

Try number two.

It rang through to a recording at the Utah FBI Office.

I hesitated before I hit the icon for the third number. What if it wasn't Brad's number? People move all over the country and keep their same cell number. Was I going to keep trying and waking up people in the middle of the night until I found the right number? Of course, I was. I pressed the next one.

"Trace, what the hell is going on, now?"

"Is this Brad Hughes?"

"Who the hell is this?" He sounded shocked as well as irritated.

At least, he hadn't asked if I knew what time it was. "Ensley Markus, I'm —"

"Trace's truck thief."

Technically, I'd borrowed Brad's fancy FBI truck. I'd driven it at over a hundred miles an hour, but, hey, I'd been in a hurry. It seems men around here are very protective of their trucks. Who knew? "Jack is missing. I found a dead body in his house, and I'm talking to you on his cell phone." Okay, he knew the cell phone part. "He's been kidnapped."

"How the hell did you get on his phone?"

"We found it at his house."

He was quiet for a few seconds. "What's with you two? You are aware these things don't happen to ordinary people." I heard rustling in the background, then a muffled voice. "Go back to sleep, honey, it's okay," he said. "How long's he been gone?" I heard a door close on his end.

"Since midnight." I tightened my grip on the phone. "The words, 'We have him.' were written in blood on the wall at Jack's."

I heard Phyllis gasp. I couldn't look at her. I had to stay strong.

"I can be there in two hours. Maybe less." There was another long pause, then he asked, "Who are *we?*" He stopped. He'd been struggling with something. Probably clothes. "Who's with you?"

I took a deep breath and ended up gasping. I walked toward Don. "Phyllis, the office manager, and Don March. He's with —"

"Crap on a cracker. What's he doing in Idaho?"

"There's more. Don was sending Jack to exchange money for information."

"Let me talk to him." That sounded like an order. I don't take orders well, but in this case, I'd let it slide.

"Brad Hughes wants to talk to you." I handed the phone to Don.

"Don March." He scowled down at me. "It's classified. You won't be needed. Homeland will be here in a few hours — I understand kidnappings are under the FBI, but this is Trace. He's under —" Don gave an irritated sigh through his clenched jaw. "Yes, I'm aware of who you are. No, of course, we can use the help." He pushed end. "Why'd you call him?"

I drew myself up and added a couple of inches by standing on my toes. "I thought it would be best to have someone here who was actually interested in finding Jack. Besides me."

We glared at each other. Don shoved Jack's phone at me and walked away.

Back out in the main area, I slumped down in one of the office chairs. Lois came over and put her head on my knee. I slid from the chair to the floor. She snuggled her head into my neck as if to hide from reality. The tan walls of the room felt as if they were closing in on me. On the one facing me, someone had fashioned a Christmas tree out of strings of green garland. Inside was a dance of multi-colored lights. Along the front wall beneath the high windows, cardboard candy canes dangled from red and green ribbons above the file cabinets. To finish the theme, a large red poinsettia sat on Phyllis's desk. Someone had the Christmas spirit.

Phyllis hung up the office phone. "Oliver is on the way to Jack's. He's calling Mullen CSU."

Jack's phone rang.

Chapter Four

A t the sound of Jack's phone, Don came over to Phyllis' desk. My hand shook as I pressed answer. "Ensley, Brad. The airport in Jackson is closed. A massive storm is dumping snow all over the mountains. Worse, it's headed your way. I'm checking the Boise airport, but if the snow is that bad in Jackson, I'm afraid the pass will be closed from that way too. I'll be there as soon as I can. I'll call you." We hung up.

Jack's phone went dark.

"What?" Don asked.

"They can't get here. A big storm is coming. I wouldn't count on your Homeland people either."

Phyllis slumped against her desk. "What're we going to do?"

I turned to Don. We had only one chance, and *that* chance didn't care if Jack lived or died. I compartmentalized the situation. It's a survival mechanism most military kids develop. You learn early to leave friends behind when you moved to the next duty station. You know your old friends will stay in touch for a while. In the end, it becomes an out of sight out of mind thing. New people come, and everyone moves on. In a few months, you put their memory in a box in your mind and set them on a back shelf. It may sound harsh, but if you didn't, you'd end up a dazed blob of emotion. "What do we do first?"

"We go to Trace's. I want to make sure they're doing everything correctly." Don's words were sour.

"Phyllis, would you take care of Lois for me? Oh no, you should go home. It's Christmas Eve. I'll take her to my house."

"I'm not going anywhere —" she glared at Don — "until we find *my* sheriff. Come here, sweetie. I know where he hides your treats." She walked toward Jack's office with Lois in tow. Poor Lois, she looked as miserable as I felt.

»§«

Jack's house could grace the cover of *Dream Home Magazine*. The two-story brick structure has the sleek lines of thoughtful design. Not something picked out of a book of 1001 house plans. We walked up the sandstone steps, across the snow covered tumbled brick patio, to the elegant glass front door.

The gorgeous wreath Jack and I had picked out and hung on his door now lay in the snow. The lush evergreen boughs are sprinkled with red frosted cranberries and white and gold holly leaves. With twists of gold ribbon here and there. The wreath is perfection. He'd objected to it, saying it was too girly. I'd informed him there was nothing feminine about pine and cranberries. I'd also pointed out there wasn't a bow anywhere on it, so his masculinity was safe. The memory made me smile despite the circumstances. I picked it up, shook off the snow, and hung it back on the door.

We found Luke Johnson, one of the CSU technicians in the living room. I'd become well acquainted with him in October during all the deaths and break-ins at the B&B. "Luke, have you found anything?"

"Hi, Doctor Markus. This is bad." He motioned for me to follow him. "We found another body on the patio off the living room." He leaned in. "Who's he?" Luke indicated Don.

"Don March, he's CIA."

Don had moved past us and was examining the body on the small side patio. "Did you see this?" he called.

We joined Don kneeling by the dead man.

He held up the man's shirt. Tattooed on his chest were crossed swords over a book with Arabic letters below.

"What does it mean?" Luke leaned over to get a better look.

"ISIS," was all Don said. He glanced up at me.

"Terrorists." He had to be part of the group Don was sending Jack to meet. I was right, radicals had him. How would they know to come here? Don was holding something back. "Is there anything to tell us where they took Jack?"

"All we found was this." Luke held out a receipt in a red-topped plastic evidence bag. "We found it on the body." He indicated the man in front of us.

"I'll take it." Don grabbed the envelope before I saw it.

"It's a receipt for The Winston Motel in Mullen," Luke told me.

"They checked out yesterday late." Don put the evidence bag in his pocket as he walked back inside. At the door, he turned. "Are you coming? I'm going to pay a visit to the motel."

"Wait," Luke called. "You can't take that, it's evidence."

"I'll return it." Without another word, Don left.

Luke hurried after Don. "It's part of the chain of evidence. You're not taking it. I could lose my job." He reached for the bag.

Don reached in his pocket and pulled out his badge. "I have the authority to take whatever I want."

Luke wasn't buying it. "I don't care if you are CIA, you're not taking my evidence."

The audible sigh that came from Don held exasperation. "You're just a CSI flunkey. Go gather your fingerprints."

Flunkey? I was sure the shocked look on Luke's face was mirrored on mine.

"CSU," whispered.

Don was halfway to the front door when I said, "I'll be sure you get it back." I hurried after Don. "That was rude and uncalled for. Luke is a great guy. He's one of the best at what he does."

I slid into the passenger's seat and crossed my arms.

"We need to stop at the Hot Springs and get your SUV. It's better in the snow than this sedan."

Don reached for the start button then stopped. He sat back and stared out the windshield. "The contact wasn't supposed to come here." He hesitated then angled toward me. "I'm sure the man on the patio with the ISIS tattoo was the contact."

"Why the change of heart?" Don had a motive, and I wanted to know what it was.

"I miss you. Come back to D.C., and marry me." He reached into his pocket and pulled out the engagement ring he'd given me three months ago. "We can pick-up where we left off. We'll forget about Idaho and Trace. I'll keep you safe."

"Pick up where we left off? Would that be before or after you nearly raped me?" You piece of garbage.

"I don't know what came over me. No, I do know. I couldn't bear the thought of you leaving me."

The four-karat diamond sparkled even in the dim light from the house.

"What about Beth?" Did he think I'd be able to step back into my old life and erase the last few of months? Leave everyone here behind? Forget Jack? I couldn't see that happening.

"Honey, it was a big mistake. I've realized how important you are to me. Beth didn't mean anything."

Wow, really? In the picture, it sure looked like he was having fun. Wait... "Keep me safe?" Those three words jumped out at me.

"You can't stay here. Being around Trace is dangerous. Deadly. That's a lesson you should have learned after what happened in October and again tonight."

"This is nothing more than a quiet small town." I wasn't counting Halloween. I should have.

"Life is never safe around him. Tonight's a perfect example. So was what happened to your dad. Death and torment follow Trace and rub off on everyone around him." He started the car. "Think about what's happened since you arrived here. Do you want the rest of your life to be filled with one incident after another?" He returned the ring to his pocket. "With me, you'll live in a brand-new condo, you'll have a place to wear all your beautiful clothes, and Sophia is there. Think about it. You'll be back home with your friends and me."

I had to hand it to Don, he knew which buttons to push. Oh, it wasn't the condo or the clothes, it was Sophie and her family. We drove in silence to the bar and grill. My SUV, covered with a foot of snow, sat alone in the parking lot. I hoped Lacey hadn't keyed it. It took several minutes to scrape the windows before we climbed inside.

"Mullen isn't far," I said as I started the engine. I was still trying to process what Don had said about life with Jack. Would it be like that? Was it worth it? I wasn't willing to let the option go … not just yet. I gripped the steering wheel and tried to sound nonchalant. "It won't take long to get there at three in the morning." I was wrong. The snow more than made up for the lack of farm animals and equipment that moved along the road in the fall. The snow slowed our progress to a crawl.

Spirit Springs shuts off its Christmas lights at midnight, leaving only a hand full of streetlights to illuminate downtown. The falling snow formed rainbow rings around the old-style lamps. "What are we going to do when we get to the motel?" I needed him to talk to me, if he was talking, I wouldn't be thinking about what was likely happening to Jack.

"Ask questions." Don sounded uneasy. I could almost feel him struggling to say something more.

I resisted the urge to glance over at him. He was a master at manipulating people, a quality he'd used to propel him up through the ranks at the CIA. I hoped his rise had been at least partly because of his skill as an agent and not solely due to his political prowess.

I turned onto the highway. As we passed the Gas and Gulp, the local truck stop, it began to snow harder. In this part of Idaho when it decides to snow, it gets right down to business. The flakes drove toward us like a million tiny white spears. The result was hypnotic as they appeared out of the dark night and shot through the headlights.

The storm Brad had warned me about was here.

"I miss you." Don's voice was soft and seductive. He reached over and put his hand on my shoulder. "I've been such a fool," he said. "I want, no, I need you back. I've pulled a few strings and called in some favors. The job at JPL Corp is yours if you'll come back with me. I had nothing to do with the destruction of your research. That was out of my hands. I'm sorry.

What? He'd ruined my career, and now he was giving it back to me. Really? What was I supposed to say? *Oh, gee thanks, honey. I'm so eager to go back to being your party doll. Oh, and by the way, it's fine with me if you keep your slut on the side.* Yes, color me bitter lemon yellow. Not only for the pain he'd caused my team, but more because of Sophie. She still hadn't found a job. The rest had.

I figured I might as well get it all out. "And by the way, no matter what you say now, we both know I wasn't important to you. I heard you tell a man I was your arm candy, someone to take to a party. Do you have any idea how I felt hearing those words? I wasn't anything more to you than a *decoration*. I wasn't someone you cared about. What made it worse, you'd already asked me to marry you."

I remembered a comment I'd overheard at a party back in D.C., Only a week after Don proposed to me, a man had asked Don where he'd found such a beautiful woman. He wanted one too. I'd heard Don laugh and say, "You mean my party favor? She does look good on my arm. She's not bad in bed either."

The man chuckled. "I'll bet she is. Can I take a shot at that?"

"Go find your own. This one is great for my career. I'm marrying her."

Those words shot home that I was nothing more to him than an accessory he took out in public to complete his image. His comment hurt on two levels; it reinforced my poor judgment with men, but more I felt cheap and used.

This wasn't Don's style. I knew there were plenty of women back east who'd love to be his arm candy. Maybe he wouldn't destroy their careers or cheat on them. So, why did he now want to make it right?

My hands ached as I gripped the steering wheel tighter.

I focused on the road.

Not on Don.

Not on the situation.

Just the road.

The Mullen coffers were obviously fuller than the ones in Spirit Springs. Here the Christmas lights here were still on. The bright red, green and gold frolicked across the bridge leading to the town beyond. I could see the glow from the lights of the Winston Motel across the bridge. Some memories are whispers, and some are screams. The memory of the pure terror I'd felt shrieked back to me. This was the spot where a couple of months ago I'd faced down two EMTs intent on murdering Jack. I could almost see the ambulance speeding toward me as I stood with my gun raised. I'd held my ground in the middle of the highway waiting and hoping, and not knowing if Jack was still alive.

I craved the feeling of happiness that should come with Christmas. Family and friends together. Instead, I felt the same dread I'd felt in October. Losing the kind of job, I'd worked my whole life to get, having to leave people who were like — no, they were family. They'd chosen to fold me into their number. Then there was the cruelest blow of all... my dad's death. Would those few days ever fade to black and white?

After all that, Jack had come into my life. I prayed I'd be in time, again.

What kind of evil does it take to kidnap someone on Christmas Eve?

The lighted motel sign appeared out of the wall of white and darkness. A huge wreath-circled the vacancy sign of the generic motel. Typical to the area, it was an enclosed two-story affair with all the doors opening onto an interior corridor. The outside was shaped concrete block with river rock accents. The exterior was dotted with standard motel windows. I parked by the entry. A sign by the sidewalk read, "Caution, snow may slide off roof."

We left the warmth of the car and walked to the entrance. The automatic doors swished open revealing an equally standard lobby. One wall held a dark wood front desk between two decorative stone partitions. Opposite the counter, set a full-sized Christmas tree. The fake tree and decorations should have been thrown out two years ago.

Tiny pink flowers and green leaves dotted the brown upholstery on the chairs. Fleetingly, I wondered how many thousands of the same chairs and tables the chain ordered at one time. However, many it was, this place needed a new table. This one appeared to have been glued back together. Twice.

Don hit the call bell on the counter so hard it bounced. Behind the front desk on a stone wall, in bronze letters, was the name Winston Motel. A minute later a sleepy-eyed man in his early twenties yawned as he walked up to the counter. His crooked nametag read 'Jimmy.' "Good evening, would you like a room?"

"We need information about some people who checked out yesterday," Don demanded.

"I can't give that out." Jimmy stood firm.

Don took out his CIA credentials and flipped them open. "This is urgent. A man was kidnapped earlier this morning." He shifted, so his jacket opened showing the butt of his gun.

Don presented an intimidating figure.

The clerk watched Don with anxiety filled eyes. Jimmy tugged at his brown clip-on tie so hard it nearly came off in his hand. "They'll fire me. I can't —"

"Son, a man's life is at stake."

The six-year difference in our ages stretched out between Don and me. Those years had me thinking of the clerk as a guy and Don thinking of him as a kid.

Jimmy's eyes bulged with fear. "I've got to call my boss."

Don stepped closer to the counter. For an instant, I thought he'd reach out and grab Jimmy by the shirt. "We don't have time. Tell me about the two men who were in this room." He slid the evidence bag across the desk. "Unless you'd like to spend your youth in federal prison for obstruction."

In the dark at Jack's, I hadn't seen the receipt at all. Bloodstains soiled the paper.

Jimmy's Adam's apple bobbed up and down as he swallowed hard. "Yes, sir." He moved to the terminal behind the counter. "I don't have much." We could see the screen. "Only their names and addresses. The usual stuff."

Don wrote down the information. "Do you have surveillance cameras?"

"Yes, sir." He tugged at his tie. This time, it came off. "They've been broken for a week."

Don took out his cell phone, pressed a couple of buttons then turned it toward Jimmy. "This one of the men?"

Jimmy's mouth fell open. "Is he dead?"

"Yes. Is he one of them?"

Jimmy managed a nod as his face grew pale.

Don swiped to the next picture. "And this one?"

Another nod. Jimmy's complexion now mirrored the color of the snow outside.

"Thank you." Don walked to the door. "Coming?" he said to me.

Outside, I said, "You scared him half to death."

"It worked, didn't it?"

It had, but I figured we could have gotten the same information with a lot less intimidation. "If those names aren't phony, and the credit card isn't stolen, it'll be a miracle," I said as we got back in the car.

"Won't matter." He pulled his phone from his pocket. "It's the little things, the automatic ones I'm hoping they overlooked —" Into his phone, he said, "Don March. Clearance number A5595JB7. Run this information." He read the two names and gave the license plate number. "The plate first. No, it's a rush. Call me as soon as you have something."

"What now?" I was in no mood to hang around doing nothing. "Should I call Brad Hughes and give him the information, too?"

"If it makes you happy." His manner was still borderline dismissive. As if he were talking to someone who didn't have the full picture or the capacity to understand it if they did. Don hadn't changed.

I pulled Jack's phone from my pocket, pressed Brad's number. I gave him the same information.

"I'm sorry. They've closed the roads into your area in both directions. I don't know if we'll be able to get to you today. Tomorrow isn't shaping up any better. It all depends on when the snow stops." I felt the regret I heard in his voice. "I'll run the plate and let you know." He paused. "You call me with anything. I'll be here."

"Thank you." No one was coming. Don was it.

Brad cleared his throat. "If I can find any way — any way at all, I'll be there. Keep in touch."

"Thanks, Brad. I'll call if there's a change." We hung up. "Jane."

"What?" Don stared at me.

"Jane. I promised her I'd call." I pulled out my cell this time.

She picked up on the first ring.

I told her what we'd found and what we'd done.

"I'm going to call Stan."

"He'll only worry." I paused. Uncle Stan only gave nicknames to those he cared a great deal for. I had one, my brother Cole had one, and Jack had one. "On second thought, call him, I don't know what he can do, but he should know what's going on."

"I will, right now."

"Tell him we're doing everything we can," I said. "With this storm, I don't know if he's going to be able to get here for Christmas. I don't know about the Boise airport, but the Jackson airport is closed. So is the one in Driggs. The airports don't matter because all the roads into this area are closed." I held the phone with both hands as if I could glean some warmth from it.

Jane made me promise to be careful and to call. We hung up. It wasn't a bad idea for her to call Uncle Stan. He was one of the three men Don had accused of... what? Other than they'd supposedly made their fortunes from *it*. Whatever *it* was.

"Don, we can't sit here hoping a computer somewhere will come up with what we need."

"I still don't have any contacts here," he said.

"Wait." I got out and hurried back inside. Don followed. "Hi, Jimmy." I smiled at him, hoping it would erase some of Don's intimidation. "Have you seen the guys we asked about other than at the motel?"

"Yeah." He held onto the edge of the counter. "I saw them at the store on Saturday. They had a bunch of snack stuff, some colored nylon rope and a couple of cases of pop. I figured they were getting ready to hit the road. But, they didn't leave until yesterday." He'd answered a little too quickly.

"Thank you. You've been very helpful," I said.

Jimmy glanced up at Don. "He's not going to arrest me, is he?" he whispered.

"No."

Don rolled his eyes.

Back in the car, I said, "Interesting."

"It might mean a lot of things. Your scared little friend would have told us Martians were in room 109 to get us out of there." He watched the snow gather on the hood of my SUV. "This weather changes things."

"Wait, they're local. The plate number is from this county." I took a shuddering breath. "Do you realize how much area is out there? Desert filled with miles and miles of nothing but grass, rocks, and sand. Now it's under several feet of snow, we can't even get to most of the ranches." I leaned back, letting my head fall against the headrest. "At least they aren't your terrorists."

"Don't be too sure."

Last night on the news, they'd said we were in for snow. Too bad they hadn't mentioned it was coming in the form of a hundred-year blizzard. "Of course, if no one can get in, no one can get out. With this weather, whoever has Jack has to be close by."

A gust of wind rocked the SUV sending a curtain of snow into the air. I sat there, in a storm, with my ex-fiancé trying to find my, what? What exactly were Jack and I to each other?

Out of the blue, Don reached for me. "I love you."

I shied away.

"I have to say this." He exhaled and let his hand drop. "I'm … I'm so sorry. I knew you were leaving me. I thought if you had no other choice, you'd stay with me."

And... he'd skipped right over the whole cheating and near rape thing. The console separated us. Thank God. The snow swirled up around the parking lot lights. I struggled to sort out my thoughts and emotions. I wasn't any good to anyone if I got caught up in a useless battle with Don. I needed to focus on my goal. Finding Jack.

Jack's phone rang startling me. "Hello."

"Doctor Markus? It's Phyllis." I could hear her as she took a sobbing breath. "Something horrible just happened. They pitched a rock through the window. There's something tied to it —" She wept — "and it's all bloody."

"We're on our way. Call Luke." I trembled as I hit the start button then seized the gearshift. I slammed the car into reverse. It skidded, nearly taking out two vehicles.

"Let me drive." Don's voice was unruffled. "We're not going to get anything done if we're stranded in a ditch freezing to death." We changed places. "Who was on the phone?" he asked as he calmly drove out of the parking lot.

Chapter Five

A CSU vehicle occupied one of the parking spaces in front of the Sheriff's Office.

I stepped out into the deepening snow. The wind thrashed against the building, sending snow past me and into the broken window. Someone had taped an evidence bag over the hole. I struggled to compartmentalize everything. Unfortunately, it was getting harder and harder to cram emotions into that cubby hole in my head.

Inside, the pine garland around the entry filled the office with the fresh scent of Christmas. Phyllis sat at her desk, her back purposely toward Luke. Lois lay on the floor beside her. The Merry Christmas letters taped to the front of her desk hung loose on one end.

The sound of the jingle bells on the door brought Lois to her feet. She hurried over to me, her toenails clicking on the tile floor, and her tail wagging. I knelt and wrapped my arms around her neck. "It'll be okay. You're a good girl," I whispered. She rewarded me by sticking her nose in my ear. I kissed the top of her nose then let her go.

Luke and another CSU tech were hunched over one of the desks. "Luke," I called.

He straightened and silently faced me. As he did, he blocked the item on the desk.

"What ... what is it?" My imagination had been spinning since we'd left Mullen. In my mind's eye, I'd seen everything from Jack's bloody hand to his still-beating heart tied to the rock. Rational thought had played no part in any of it.

"It doesn't make sense." Luke stepped aside. "It's not a ransom note."

A rock lay on the gray composite surface of the desk. Beside it, a note spattered with blood.

Don took out a pen and slid the note around to face him. "How long ago did this happen?"

"I called Doctor Markus right after." Phyllis came over. Her bright red sweater had a fuzzy green and white Christmas tree knitted into the front of it. The tiny silver bells dotted around the tree should have made a happy noise. Instead, they sounded tinny.

The bloody yellow sheet read: *He will pay for his crimes.*

"It's crudely printed," Don pointed out. "Probably to disguise the handwriting." I heard the hesitation in his voice.

I couldn't take my eyes from the words. "What crimes?"

"Not here." To the CSU technicians, Don asked, "What facilities do you have?"

Luke bit his lip as if to hold back a remark that wouldn't help the situation. "A small lab," he said. "We do the basics and send the complicated stuff to Boise."

Don dropped the evidence bag with the receipt in it on the desk. He wrote his cell number on one of his cards and handed it to Luke. "How long will this take?"

"The sheriff is our priority."

I pulled my gaze from the desktop and focused on Luke's face. "Do you know a guy named Jimmy? He works at the Winston Motel."

"Yeah. He dated my sister a couple of times last summer."

"What do you think of him?"

He gave a one shoulder shrug. "He's okay."

"Nothing stands out about him?" I asked.

"Besides he's a loser. No. Why?"

"We talked to him earlier," I angled around so Luke blocked what lay on the desk. "Is he trustworthy?"

"I didn't like him much. He's taking online classes in accounting, I think."

"Thanks. If you come up with anything —" I couldn't finish. I couldn't make the words form in my mind.

Luke's mouth tightened into a grim line. "I'll do my best for the sheriff." He regarded Don. "And you," he whispered.

"I want a copy of the note," Don ordered.

Luke's nod was almost a salute. "I'll let you know what we find out." He looked at Don's card before he put it in his pocket then went to make a copy.

Don left the central area and entered Jack's office. The room sits in the center of the larger space. The top two-thirds of the three walls are glass. The bottom is regular wall. Through the open louvered wooden blinds, I could see Don standing where Jack should be.

I leaned against Phyllis's desk. On the opposite corner, a bowl molded in the shape of a Santa head sat half empty. The brightly wrapped Christmas candy dulled in the early morning despair. "What do you know about Jack?"

"Rumor has it you know him a lot better than I do." Her smile had a gossipy flare about it.

There was nothing to know. "Don't believe everything you hear." The grapevine in Spirit Springs rivals the internet for speed and accuracy. They both get it right about half the time, with some outlets more reliable than others. I figured Phyllis had the inside track. "I mean before he came here."

She glanced down at Lois. "Not much. He doesn't like to talk about himself." I heard … no felt her hesitancy to say whatever came next. She knew a lot more than she was willing to tell me.

I knew he'd been an Army medic. It had come in handy when we were stranded on the mountain south of town last fall. His skills were good, but what saved us was his fully stocked Army aid bag. When I'd asked what he'd done in the Army, I'd gotten a cryptic, 'my job.' It's a typical response from guys who didn't want to or weren't able to talk about what they'd done. I figured it had a lot more to do with him being Delta Force.

I watched Don as he stood behind Jack's desk moving papers

around. His posture reminded me of when I'd seen him standing next to Jack at the bar last night. It felt like a million years ago. Their faces, coloring, and mannerisms were different, but if they'd been in silhouette, I wouldn't be able to tell them apart. I must have a physical type. Okay, seriously? Who wouldn't want a tall, strong, well-built guy? They're both alphas, both in incredible shape, and both great looking. Okay, Jack was a lot more handsome, but then, I wasn't entirely unbiased.

What had brought these two opposite men together? Were they as different as they seemed?

"Doctor Markus?" Luke drew my attention.

"Ensley, please." I figured we should be on a first name basis.

"Ensley, I have everything. I'll process this as fast as I can. Everyone is off for Christmas, so it's just me and Carl there. He's new but pretty good."

"Thank you," I knew the smile I gave him was feeble.

"You're going to find him, aren't you?" Phyllis put her hand on my arm.

"I don't know how to do this alone." Alone. The word echoed in my mind. For the first time since I'd been in Spirit Springs, I felt alone. In D.C., loneliness hadn't been a stranger. The only close friend I had was Sophie, my research assistant. Sophie and I did a lot together; we ran three times a week, and we'd gone on vacation together. I ate Sunday dinner with her family. The Bianchi's all insisted I was now one of them. If I didn't call Mama on Sunday, she called first thing Monday morning to enquire where to send flowers because I was either in a coma or dead. Those were the only excuses she'd accept.

No, the loneliness came when I'd been with Don. I don't know why it took me so long to figure it out.

"You've got him." Luke indicated Don.

"I do." I hoped Don would turn out to be more helpful than he'd been so far. I hoped he was doing his best right now, and his desire for me to go back to D.C., with him wasn't standing between what he wanted and what I needed.

"I've got to get these back to the lab."

"Thanks." I knew the smile I gave him held more gloom than cheer, but it was the best I could manage.

Luke left, and Phyllis went to her desk as — Jack's phone rang. "Hello?"

"Ensley. Brad. The license plate number you gave me comes back to Max Jessen. I've checked, and his wife is still in Boise. She's trying to get the judge to reconsider bail for him. No chance I'll let that happen."

"Whoever has Jack threw a rock with a note attached to it through the window of the police station." The desk where the CSU techs had been sat empty. "It says, 'He will pay for his crimes.' It's bloody." I waited a beat, not sure if I should ask the next question. I knew one thing, the man on the phone had known Jack for a long time. Now, did I have enough left in me to hear his answer? I walked away from Phyllis's desk. "What crimes are they talking about?"

Silence.

I gripped the phone with both hands. "Please, Brad."

"He hasn't committed any. You know he's not that kind of man."

"I do." The words slipped out softly betraying my lack of confidence. It wasn't that I believed Jack was a criminal, it was more my dismal history judging men's character.

"He's turned down assignments he thought were unethical." Brad laughed. "He has a reputation, and they don't —" I could hear the oh-shit in his pause. "Let's just say it's a problem sometimes. Not for him, but those in charge. The ones who are always sure they know what's best for everyone." He chuckled. "I love it when they're wrong, and he tells them so just before he says no."

"I need to know who we're dealing with." There was no logic to any of this. "One of the dead men at Jack's had a terrorist tattoo on his chest. Don told me he was sending Jack on an exchange with an operative who'd infiltrated a radical group. Could they be the one's holding him?"

A long deep silence stretched between us. Finally, he said, "Let me speak to March." His voice held a stiff, formal note. I pictured him standing at attention.

I walked into Jack's office and held out Jack's phone. "Brad Hughes wants to talk to you."

Don frowned as he took the phone from me. "March. — I know perfectly well what the directive says. This is a unique circumstance. Hold on — I don't appreciate being — go right ahead. I received special permission. *Do not* talk to me like I'm —" Don pulled the phone away from his ear and shoved it at me. "You talk to him."

"Hello?" I walked out of the office and back to Phyllis's desk.

"That piece of garbage is not supposed to have any control over Jack. I'm. Seriously. Pissed. Off." I heard him take an angry breath. "I don't trust March to do the right thing. Personal history aside, don't you trust him, either."

"I don't know how to do this on my own, I can't find Jack without him." I wanted to believe Don *would* do the right thing. "Are these people we're dealing with from Jack's past?" Don was part of mine.

"Those who would want to punish Jack are either in a place where they won't be doing anyone harm, or they're dead." He paused. "Or I know where they are. This has a local feel to it, despite the tattoo or March." I heard the apprehension in his voice. "Still..."

"You know more. Who are these men?"

"I need to check on something. I'm going to wake up a few people. I'll let you know what I find out."

With another promise to stay in contact, we said goodbye

Don was on his phone. It was so foreign seeing him here. Our small town wasn't his world. I knew he used to be an agent, but that's not who he was now. He'd given up the covert life for one of politics, back room deals, and parties. He'd traded his undercover existence for one on the society pages. I was sure the old Don March wasn't much different than the one standing in Jack's office. He was as ruthless as Jack was compassionate.

At parties, he'd demanded admiration. He got it by making clandestine deals, and I'd almost bet there was blackmail mixed in there for added insurance. I'd seen Don *convince* someone to come around to his way of thinking. He'd do whatever it took to get what he wanted.

Jack demanded nothing. I'd seen the look on his face as he pulled the trigger killing two men. I knew what it had cost him, and the reason he'd do it again if he had too. He wanted to make things right.

The catalyst in this whole situation was Don's arrival. Why had he come all the way out here? Oh, sure, he said he wanted to tell me in person about getting my job back and to ask me to take him back and marry him. Then there was this mission he had for Jack. If those were the reasons, he'd only addressed one of them. What about the informant? Anyone could make the exchange. Why Jack? Why didn't Don have a backup plan? Jack always had a plan 'B.'

"Ensley," Don called as he reached for his jacket and headed for the door. He motioned for me to join him. "Let's go."

"Phyllis, I'll call you if we find anything."

"I'll do the same," she assured me.

I bent down and gave Lois a hug. Her sad golden eyes appeared as lost and confused as I felt.

The cluster of gold jingle bells on the front door clanked against the glass as it closed behind me.

Outside, I got into the passenger's seat. "Where are we going?"

"We're headed for Max Jessen's ranch. Do you know where it is? I have directions if you don't."

"It's half an hour out on a good day. With this storm, it'll take forever to get there. I talked to Brad, and the Jessens are all still in Boise."

"I know. That's the reason we're going."

"We won't make it in my car. Especially if it keeps snowing like this. We've got to go get Jack's truck."

"We'll be fine." His sharp tone had me glancing over at him.

Oh, please, he knew better. The last thing I wanted was to get stranded with Don. "Not if we're stuck out in the snow, in the country, freezing to death. The scenario he'd come up with earlier was worth repeating. This SUV doesn't have the clearance we'll need. Jack's big truck has snow tires, and it sits a lot higher than mine does."

He turned down the road to Jack's house.

The wind blustered through the trees, sending the already fallen snow back into the air. It almost covered the gracefully weeping evergreens by the sandstone steps. The windows were all dark. It made the house appear desolate, abandoned. I reminded myself I'd only known Jack for ten weeks.

His phone in my pocket weighed a thousand pounds. The first night I'd met him he'd held this phone, pressing the buttons so the lights would be on when I got to his house. A total stranger to me. He knew Dad and Uncle Stan very well. Maybe they were the reasons he'd been so kind in the beginning. They weren't the reason now. I swallowed the tears at the back of my throat as I wrapped my arms around me.

"Ensley do —" he stopped and reached for my hand. "Are you, all right?"

I pulled away. "Of course, I'm not *all right*. This is overwhelming." My stability quotient was down past the critical level. "All I want is to find Jack and you to leave. Don, there's nothing you can do to get me to go back with you. My home is here now. I don't want the job at JPL. I don't want to live in D.C. This is the first time in my adult life I've felt at home." That wasn't strictly true. I felt at home when I was with Sophie and her family.

He remained silent as he parked the SUV next to the garage door. He didn't look at me, he just glared at the garage. "Do you know where the keys are?"

"Keys. Yes. Around the side." The cold assaulted me as I got out of my SUV and went to the planter next to the side door. Between the fight and the CSU techs, the snow was trampled. Only a thin new blanket of snow covered the sheltered area off the living room. Luke and Carl had taken the body away. I imagined I could still see the blood stain on the bricks. A shuddering sigh betrayed me. This was the same patio where I'd made a drunken pass at Jack on a chilly October night. I smiled. It had almost worked. He'd had the honor and the good sense to say no. I fished the key out of a planter.

Inside, I went to the pantry and plucked the extra set of truck keys from a bowl.

"The garage is this way." I motioned down the hall.

When we left, I secured the house and set the alarm.

"Been here often?" Don asked as the garage door slid open.

"Of course I have."

"I know how he operates."

"Not now."

"You need to know he's not the man you think he is."

Chapter Six

Jack's cell rang. I didn't check to see who it was. I didn't care, and it didn't matter, it would be a random string of numbers and letters. "Hello," I said as I got in the truck and shut the door.

"Ensley, Brad. I've been sitting here being pissed at the weather and annoying some people with my phone calls. I have something. Have you heard of a couple by the name of Sharp, Shaver, or Shaw?"

"The Shaws?" I thought about them. I didn't care for them, but you don't have to like your guests if they pay their bill and don't steal or destroy things. "Yes, they stayed at the B&B for a couple of days. Why?"

Don got in the truck and slammed the door.

"It seems Max Jessen's daughter uses all three names," Brad was saying. "What did they look like?"

"I have her picture here. She's ordinary, medium build, chin-length standard brown hair, and flat brown sunken eyes. The kind of person you'd walk by and not notice. The husband is lean with slimy black hair and watery blue eyes. Oh, and his nose looks like it was broken and not set properly."

"Sounds like them. My contact said they left Boise on Wednesday."

"That's the day they checked in. It was a last-minute reservation." I slumped against the seat as Don started the truck. "But it can't be his daughter. She's in prison."

"One is, one isn't. The one who's out is more dangerous than the one who's in. She's a problem all by herself, but pair her up with her bat-shit-crazy husband, and it's time to lock up the kids and small animals. We're talking a torture-little-creatures-and-bury-them-in-the-backyard psychopath. I got a call a few minutes ago, and the snow is letting up in Jackson. If it holds, they'll get the runway plowed. If the pass opens, I'll be there. I've got some men coming from Boise, too. I hope they can get there as soon as the storm lets up."

If they were Brad's men, it meant they had experienced finding kidnapped victims. "Are they your men?'

"In a way," was all he said.

Interestingly vague for a man who is nothing if not straight forward. Don backed out of the garage. Here the snow showed no sign of letting up. If anything, it was coming down harder. There had to be easily a foot and a half of new snow since Don showed up on my doorstep.

"I know how tough Jack is. How could a few amateurs overpower him?"

"They couldn't, that's what's troubling. Crazy and company are no match for him armed or unarmed. Let me talk to March."

Their conversation hadn't gone well the last time. But I'm ever the optimist. I handed the phone to Don. "Brad would like to speak to you."

"Hughes again," he said as he took the phone.

"Yes."

"Great." Into the phone, he said, "Now what?"

I could imagine Brad's response.

"No. I had nothing to do with his kidnapping, and I resent the accusation." Don paused. "My contact couldn't possibly be involved. — He has no idea who was coming to make the exchange. — I'll see what I can find out." Don tossed the phone back to me.

I had no idea what to say. If Don had anything to do with this, I'd... I don't know... shoot him. To Brad, I said, "We've got to find out who we're up against. If they're like the men in October, we won't be any match for them." Don was no Jack.

"We'll find him," Brad hesitated then said, "I know how much you mean to him."

How'd Brad know? I didn't. Oh, I knew Jack cared. He'd held me in his arms and kissed me, but he'd never taken it any further. I wasn't ready for more; I was still off balance. Today, I should be wrapping gifts, putting cookies on a Christmas plate and enjoying Jack's company. Instead, I was searching for him in a horrible storm. All I knew was, I had to find him before it was too late. "Thanks, Brad." I couldn't keep the fear from my voice. What if I was already too late?

"Wait, I have more. Daughter number two made threats against everyone involved in the resort case. Mostly you and Jack."

He was talking about my dad's case. "I know about the threats. But people say things in moments of stress they never follow through on. When nothing happened, I thought it was all over." Outside the snow fell with such vigor, I couldn't see half a block ahead.

"We all did. Tell me you're not going to the Jessen place."

I didn't say anything.

"When you do, do not go alone. Do you hear me? Take someone with you. Several someone's. I don't know who is out there. The man on Jack's patio with the Islamic tattoo worries me. I'm waiting for a call. When I get it, a lot of questions will be answered."

"Don is with me. We can stop and pick up —"

"Let me speak to him," Brad demanded. There was a lot of that tonight... this morning.

I held out the phone to Don. "He wants to talk to you again." There was a dynamic going on here I didn't understand. I knew Jack was Delta Force — or had been — because of the medallion on the keychain he'd given me. Don appeared to be in charge of Jack, yet Brad said he wasn't supposed to be. Brad seemed to be able to tell Don what to do, but Brad was FBI and Don was CIA. All very confusing.

"Great." He put the phone to his ear as he slowed to take a corner. "Yes. I'm quite capable." His voice was as stiff as his posture. "I'm aware of — I don't appreciate being —" Don pushed the end bar. For a split second, I thought he'd crush the phone, my lifeline to Jack. As always, he regained his composure. "Nice friends you have out here." He dropped the phone in my lap.

"Brad told me the Shaws, a couple who were staying at the B&B, may be responsible for Jack's kidnapping," I explained about Max's two daughters, the one in prison and one free. "If Brad's right and I'm sure he is, we've got to find Jack." It occurred to me. "There were just the two dead men on the receipt from the motel?"

"Yes. Why?"

"I'm trying to figure out what we're up against." I shook my head. "All I know for sure is, we have two dead bodies and the Shaws. It would take more than one man and one woman to overpower Jack."

"Trace must be slipping in his old age. He should have been able to handle a bunch of untrained civilians."

Nice compassion. I didn't look at Don. It would only make me angrier. Not looking didn't work. "Why are you helping me find Jack? And don't tell me it's the exchange. Because you said that time has passed."

"No. Not yet. I still have a chance to make it myself. The problem is the kidnappers took the cash I brought for my informant."

Don turned the truck toward the police station. "We need some weapons."

"You don't care if we find him, do you?"

"No."

I sat there stunned. I knew these two didn't like each other, but this was so much *more* than a professional rivalry. *More* than I'm going to get even. Much *more*. This hatred went deep on Don's side. I knew Jack didn't have any use for Don, but he'd never expressed this level of animosity. By the front door of the sheriff's office sat one of the official trucks.

"Maybe Oliver's here," I said. "We should take him with us." Bringing along an ally sounded like an excellent idea to me.

"Oliver?"

"He's one of Jack's deputies. Nice man."

"We don't need nice," Don said as he parked. "We need experience. I'm not taking some Barney Fife along to bungle things."

"Don —" What? I figured pointing out he was an ass wouldn't

solve anything. "We can't go alone. They took Jack, but only after he killed two of them."

"I'm aware of his skills." He shut off the truck. "I've been in the field. I know how to take care of myself."

My cell rang again. "Hello." I didn't get out of the truck.

"Boss, you haven't called. I'm worried."

"Oh, Jane, I'm so sorry." She'd been around the Shaws more than I had. "What do you think of the Shaws."

"He had a mean side to him. I caught him trying to kick little Mattie. I was set to throw them out when Mrs. Shaw came along and apologized. She said he had a fear of cats. I didn't buy it, but since they were leaving later, I let it go and took Mattie with me." I could imagine a full-grown man kicking my slash our little seven-pound kitty hadn't set well. "Mrs. Shaw wasn't very friendly. Real touchy, kind of a chip on her shoulder attitude. I kept thinking something was familiar about her. I still can't put my finger on it. It's been bothering me."

"What if I told you she was Max Jessen's daughter?"

"He only has the one. She's in jail," Jane's words were slow as if she were pondering the idea.

"Brad Hughes told me he has another one."

After a few seconds, Jane said, "Hm. Back before he married, he ran with a girl from down to Driggs. He quit bringing her around. Everyone figured she got smart and dumped him. She may have gotten pregnant. The child would be about Mrs. Shaw's age."

"Have you been in their room since they left?"

"I'm heading up now. I haven't cleaned. I was getting things ready for Christmas Day. What do you want me to look for?"

I turned to Don. "She's in the Shaws's room. Where should she search?"

"Put her on speaker. Jane, Don March. Look in the trash cans, on the desk or table, anywhere you'd find paper."

"It'll take a second," Jane said.

"I'll wait." Don positioned the phone on the dash.

I could hear her moving things around. Finally, she said, "I found some notes. They don't make any sense."

"Listen carefully. I don't want you to leave the building. You're safe there, they aren't after you." He stopped. "We'll come and get you. Right now, read what's on the paper —" Around us, the lights went out. "Hello? Hello?" He handed me Jack's phone.

"The power failure must have affected the cell tower, too." At least, we had the radio in Jack's truck. "Let's go get Jane."

"She'll be fine." Don opened the truck door.

"No. We need to make sure she's safe." We couldn't leave her with no protection. "At least let's go get her and bring her back to the police station. It isn't far."

"They have no interest in her, or they would have taken her before now."

"We need to know what she found." Maybe that would change his mind.

Don got out of the truck.

His mind hadn't changed.

"Come on," he called.

I had to convince him to go get Jane. I'd go myself, but he had the only set of keys. "Give me the keys. I'm going after her."

"No. We'll go get her later. Right now, we have more important things to deal with."

The only thing more important than going to get Jane was finding Jack. I turned and walked toward the B&B. I'd made the CHECK block trip lots of times. "I'll go check on her myself."

The response I got was swift and fierce.

Don spun me around. "No. You're. Not." The instant he did, he realized he'd overreacted and let go of me. "Are you giving up on Trace?" He took a half step back. "Think about this logically. They have what they want, they aren't going to risk coming out of their hiding place to get your friend."

It made sense. The problem was, bad guys, aren't always rational. "Brad told me Mrs. Shaw is Max Jessen's daughter," I said as I caught up with him.

"Jessen is the one who tried to kill you in October." It hadn't been a question.

I didn't like the fact he was keeping close track of me. Or, any track at all. "How do you know these things?"

"Police report."

"Jack sent you the police report?" I was sure that hadn't been voluntary. I knew Don had requested a copy of my dad's case file be given to me last fall. I didn't see information flowing in Don's direction willingly. Especially, after Don's confession that he didn't care if we found Jack.

I decided Don had someone inside Jack's office, someone feeding him information. The only person who'd been disloyal was Jane's nephew, Kenny. He'd ended up dead after the scandal last fall. Who could it be? Everyone else appeared loyal.

"I got it through other channels," was all he said.

The emergency lights were on inside the Sheriff's Office. Lois got to her feet as soon as the bells hit the glass front door.

Phyllis didn't wake up. I knelt beside her and touched her arm. "Phyllis, go home. I'll take Lois to my house."

She rubbed her eyes. "Doctor Markus, did you find Jack?" She rubbed her eyes.

"Ensley, please. No, we haven't found him."

"What happened? Why are the emergency lights on?" She stretched and yawned.

"The storm must have taken down a power line," I said. "We're heading out to the Jessen place. Is Oliver around?"

"He went out to recheck Jack's house. Want me to call him?"

"The cell service is out. Whose truck is out front?" Don asked.

"Oliver switched trucks. The old one was having engine trouble."

"Can you radio him?" I wanted Oliver with us.

"Yes," she reached to turn on the radio.

"No," Don said. "We'll contact him if we need him." I followed Don into Jack's office. He took a rifle and ammunition from the rack behind the desk. I wanted to stop the someone who was making my life miserable. Jack's .40 cal. would do that nicely. In the outer office, I knelt by Lois and Phyllis. "I'll bring him home." I hoped to God I could make good on my promise.

I crawled up in the truck as Don started it. "I'm better with a rifle," I said.

"You've got your .38 and whatever you took from Trace's desk. You'll be fine."

Don was nothing if not consistent. Looking at him through the lens of time, made me shutter.

After Sophie and I went for our makeovers — the one she didn't need — I felt like I was living someone else's life. Men who'd never noticed me were now asking me out, keeping me busy every Friday and Saturday night. I decided to enjoy it all while it lasted. Then a year ago my brother Cole took me to one of those *mandatory* parties. The kind no one has fun at, but everyone goes to because they have too. Cindy, his wife, was sick with the flu and Cole said he wanted someone to talk to who didn't have an agenda. Tag, I was it.

That night I met Don. I couldn't miss him, he was the one people stepped aside for as he walked toward me. He was impressive, dressed in a tux. He looked every bit the Prince Charming he wasn't.

I fastened my seatbelt and leaned back. Outside, the snow fell as if it were determined to fill the valley. I let out a sigh. It was still dark, and I was still scared.

"You know we may not find him alive."

I stared at Don. "If you think he's dead, why are you risking our lives?"

He was silent for a long minute. "I've got to make the exchange. I can't do it without the money."

The stoplight hung dark in the center of the intersection ahead.

"Is the mission more important than all our lives?"

"It isn't only the mission. It's all the people this information will save. You, of all people, should know, I'm not as unfeeling as everyone thinks. This is what I do, I make hard decisions. Decisions I have to live with." He cast a glance over at me. "You understand."

I was trying to.

Chapter Seven

In the dark and snow, we almost missed the road to the Jessen ranch. Our headlights showed a set of tire tracks turning toward the house.

"Keep going."

"I'm not a rookie," he snapped.

The valley is rolling pastureland with only an occasional tree to disrupt the bleak winter landscape. As soon as the sun came up, we'd be seen. I stared at the clock on the dash. "This isn't good. We have less than an hour before sunrise."

Don turned the truck around and shut off the lights. "We walk."

"In this weather? It'll take too long." The wind outside blew so hard the big truck rocked back and forth.

"Giving up?"

He had no idea. He may know some facts about my life, but he'd never taken the time to know the person living it. "I don't give up." I took the .40 cal. and the extra clip I'd taken from Jack's office and secured it to my waistband. I got out and opened the back door and began searching through Jack's aid bag. I smiled. He'd replaced the red space blanket from last fall. The red one had been a problem when we were stranded in the mountains. I took everything I thought I'd need and stuffed it in my pockets.

Mental note:
Get a jacket with larger or at least more pockets.

"You think you're going to need all that?"

"Yes."

"You sure?" Don pulled the collar of his coat up around his ears.

I zipped my jacket shut. "After the damage, we found at his house, you don't think we'll find him injured?"

"You should know." Disdain saturated his words.

"What's that supposed to mean?"

"You've gotten very cozy with a man you don't know much about."

He was one snarky comment away from my knee revisiting his crotch. I held my temper. "Not now."

"Then, when? Should I tell you everything now? He's an accomplished liar." He faced me. "I know how attractive he is to women. I've used his appeal on several missions. He uses his good looks to his advantage as often as he can. You should know his past isn't —"

I'd call him on this once and for all. "What kind of monster is he? I'd really like to know before I make *another* mistake." He could tell me all about Jack as we made our way to the Jessen ranch. Of course, I wouldn't hear him over the sound of the wind. That was all right with me.

Don stepped back. "I'll tell you when this is all over. Right now, if we have any chance, we've got to get to the ranch before sunrise."

This was like a game to him. First, he was eager to tell me everything. Whatever *everything* was. Then, he'd state something designed to hurt not help. I figured that was his goal. Was that the point? To hurt me more?

We walked in the truck's tire tracks back to the turnoff. The ranch looked as if it was straight out of an old western. Instead of sand and dirt, snow blew over the low-slung buildings. It had drifted so high on one side, the structures appeared to lean under the weight.

"The first outbuilding isn't far," Don called over the sound of the wind as he checked his rifle. "Get your weapon out and stay down."

I remembered the buildings from October when Jack and I'd come out to talk to the cowboy, Cid. I only knew what was in one of them. "The large one is a horse barn."

"Thanks. Stay close."

It wasn't bad walking down the tire tracks. When we left the packed surface, it proved slow going for me, at least. The snow was above my knees. "It's already starting to get light. They're going to know exactly where we are in a few minutes," I pointed out.

The first shed was empty. At least, the small building sheltered us from the raw wind. Around us, the corrugated tin of the walls and roof rattled with each gust. I wasn't sure how much longer the building could withstand the onslaught.

We made the big barn, it was warm inside. We checked each stall. Only a few had horses in them. The others held hay, feed, or tack. Nothing more. The Arabian, the one Max had bought for the daughter now in jail, whinnied at us from the first stall. As I reached out to stroke his nose to calm him, he threw his head in the air and shied away.

Don peered out the door at the paddock.

With visibility near zero, the house beyond was nothing more than a faint impression. "Let's go to the house next," I said. "It's about forty feet from here."

"Why? No one's here."

"I said so. That's why." I wasn't going to let Don intimidate me one minute more. "If they've been here, we'll see the signs."

"Maybe." He scrutinized the area between the horse barn and the house.

I went to one of the horse stalls. "Don."

"What?"

"The water in the buckets is fresh, and the horses have been fed."

He joined me. "The tire tracks were probably from one of the hands doing chores. Let's go."

I wasn't leaving without searching the house. "We're checking the house."

"No." He started towards the far end of the barn.

"They may have left something."

"Ensley, they were never here."

"Someone was here and not long ago. The tire tracks would be covered otherwise." I pulled open the door nearest the house. "Look," I pointed. "There're footprints in the snow."

He pointed to the lights. "The generator is working. If anyone was in the house, we'd see the lights."

"Maybe the windows are covered." This didn't make sense. Was he doing this on purpose? Only one way to find out. "I would think an experienced CIA operative wouldn't leave anything to chance. We need to check inside, then follow the footprints." I had to check even if he wasn't going to. I headed for the door.

"If it will get you to leave." Don went through the door first.

We trudged across the open area toward the large stone home. No one shot at us. That was a good news, bad news situation. As much as I hate being shot at, it would mean the bad guys were here. I struggled to put a few drops back in my optimism glass. At least, we'd know one place they weren't.

I thought the tire tracks had stopped at the front of the barn near the door. They didn't, still, there was no other sign of live. But with as much snow that had fallen any other tracks were covered with at least a foot and a half of snow.

Don tried the side door. It was unlocked. He flattened me back against the house. "I hate unlocked doors." He pushed it open.

Nothing blew up, and no shots were fired. He crouched down and disappeared into the darkness. A few seconds later, he flipped on the lights.

"Don't." I reached for the switch. "They'll see us."

"They aren't here. I'll prove it," he said. We searched every room in the house. Each one had the same tired, worn appearance. The whole house smelled old, dirty and sour. All the walls were in desperate need of paint. We found dirty dishes frozen in the sink. I remembered Jack telling me Max Jessen was one of the wealthiest ranchers in the area. Maybe ranchers had the same outlook on their houses they had on clothes. They only bought new when the old was past useful. This whole place was far past livable inside. So why hadn't it been replaced? I pushed aside a fallen newspaper with my foot.

Don was right, we found nothing. They weren't here. No one had been for a long while.

"Now we see where the footprints go," I said.

"This is a waste of time. We need to get back and reexamine what we have."

That seemed — I don't know, redundant. "First we see where the footprints go."

"Fine, if it will make you happy," Don closed the door to the house.

At the bottom of the steps, we followed the prints and tire marks to another outbuilding. The old barn looked as if it was original to the ranch.

Don cracked open one of the large double doors. There was no electricity in here. I pulled out my pin light. It was empty like the first building we'd entered. The only sign of a working ranch were the few horses we'd seen in the barn. "They must have sold nearly everything to pay the lawyers," I said.

I played my light around the area and found I'd been right. Everything in here had been taken away. All that was left was some broken equipment and trash. Clumps of snow had fallen off the hired hand's truck leaving the outline of his vehicle. The dirt floor was saturated with motor oil. A case must have fallen when they cleared the place out. Since it had broken open, they'd shoved it to one side.

There was nothing here. I felt disappointment steal a little more hope. I stood in the center of the area wishing for some glimmer of a clue. Anything to show us where we could find Jack.

"Now, we start over." I could hear the I-told-you-so in Don's voice as he walked to the doors.

"Where? We've examined every piece of evidence. Talked to your people and mine." Okay, technically Brad was Jack's person, but since Jack wasn't here, I claimed him. I stepped outside. I showed my small flashlight around. The round beam reflected off the falling snow, hiding everything ten feet away.

"We've got to see if the techs have anything. Do you know where the lab is in Mullen?" Don asked.

"No. If the lights are out there, too, they won't have anything."

We trudged along the road to the truck in the early morning light. I took another peek back toward the house. Where else could they be? "Before we go to Mullen, we're going back to the B&B for Jane."

"Don't worry about her. She's safe where she is."

I shook the snow from my jacket then climbed up into the passenger seat. "I want to check on her and see what she found in the Shaw's room. It would be new information." I unclipped the .40 cal. from my jeans and put the first aid supplies back in Jack's aid bag.

"It was probably nothing. It's a waste of time." He started the truck.

"Maybe, but we've searched everything else. I want to make sure Jane is okay."

Chapter Eight

I watched the driving snow and listened to the thump of the windshield wipers as they tried to beat back the never-ending barrage of snow. With every beat of the wipers and every flake that fell, I felt a little more hope drain away. I had no idea where to look next. They could be anywhere. The ranch was and wasn't the most logical place to hold Jack. Mrs. Shaw would have access to it. On the other hand, it was too obvious.

Now, what? I hated not having any idea what to do next. When this was all over, I was going to get a police procedures manual. No, *procedures* didn't sound right. I needed to know how to solve a crime. Maybe Brad would have something I could use. I wasn't going to be put in this situation again. Next time — and it was beginning to look as if this was my new normal — I'd be prepared. I'd know what to do.

Mental note:
Ask Brad about a manual.

. . .

"We'd have worked it out if you'd stayed," Don was saying. "All we needed was time to put things back together."

"What?" Was he nuts? My thoughts were like drops of water on a hot grill. As they hit the metal surface, they skittered off in all directions until they finally careened into oblivion. I turned and looked at Don as he drove. "We have more important things to concentrate on than our failed affair." Which by the way, would never have worked.

"I'm sorry for what happened." Don glanced over at me, then back at the road. "For all of it. I didn't realize until you were gone how much you meant to me. I've never felt like this in my life. I don't know what to do. Come back and be part of my life again."

I know there are a lot of people who dream of living in the limelight. Parties, seeing your picture on the society page on Sunday morning, have celebrities call you by your first name. I'd been one of those people for a while. As fantasy faded to reality, the glow of the spotlight dulled and turned hollow.

"I know I was wrong." He drove slowly toward town. "I was desperate, I couldn't let you go." He sighed. "Then you were gone."

Don had never known me at all. I was beginning to wonder if I'd known myself until I moved here. My whole existence, until I met Don, had been in the pages of a textbook. In the past few weeks, I'd become more than an unemployed doctor who'd come to town to find her father. I was now part of a community.

In D.C. I'd been just someone who rented a house and never knew her neighbors. Someone who went to work every day did her job and returned home anonymously. Even the parties Don had taken me to didn't make me feel any more included.

I belonged here now. When this was all over, and Jack was safe —

"Things will be different, I promise," Don was saying, "I told Beth I was coming here to convince you to return home with me." His smile held a hint of amusement. "Let's just say she didn't take it well."

I pushed aside the indefensible — the other woman and the near rape — and tried another approach. The parties had become a study in geopolitics and abnormal psychology. Maybe if I explained it to him, he'd understand. "I didn't want to live with the endless parties, with people I didn't know and didn't want to become involved with on any level. Besides, I hated seeing my picture on the society page."

"You were so good at it. You could charm any man in the room. With you by my side, my career would take off."

And... we were back to his career path. "What if your career ended one fall morning? Everything you'd worked on for years dumped into cartons marked 'shred.' With no hope of salvaging any of it. Your people looking to you for answers. Answers you didn't have, and all of them out of jobs. Sophie still hasn't found one."

"I had no control over your research. I told you I was wrong. What more do you want from me? I've done everything I can to make it right. Your old job is waiting for you at JPL. All you have to do is come back with me." He pulled to a halt in the middle of the country road and shoved the truck into park. For a second he glared out the windshield. Then he glanced over at me and said, "Your research is gone. I'm sorry. I didn't have anything to do with getting it pulled. It was a powerful lobby." He leaned closer. "They had JPL running scared. They panicked and fired all of you. It wasn't personal, it was business."

It felt personal. "And Beth?" I wanted to hear his explanation for the betrayal.

"I did it for you."

In what world did that make sense? "For me?"

"I thought I could get her to keep you on —"

"Hold it. You knew long enough in advance what was going to happen and you didn't tell me? You had time to go behind my back and sleep with Beth. But you couldn't find a minute to tell me my work and my career were about to be trashed?" I couldn't believe the lengths this man would go to, to get what he wanted. "I was told you were the one responsible for getting me blacklisted."

Silence.

It was a long time before he said, "I did. But when I realized what it would do to you, I went to Beth hoping to stop it. She had the power to make it all go away including saving your job. I know now, it was all a mistake. She said you deserved what you got. What did you do to her to make her hate you so much?"

71

It wasn't hate, it was revenge. I'd been stabbed in the back more than once, but Beth was the only person who actually hated me. The situation was simple in its complexity. After Sophie and I had gone for our makeovers the first man who'd asked me out was the one scientist she'd been shamelessly pursuing for months. "She thought she had a good reason." In fact, the scientist ended up marrying an accountant with large glasses and blond hair. The one who was always reading a romance novel. Maybe I should read some, after all, they were essentially about relationships. A subject I desperately needed help with.

"Ensley, don't you remember how we were together? Didn't all those months mean anything to you? All those nights?"

Guilt wasn't going to work. "Things have changed. I've changed. I'm not going back to D.C. or JPL. Research is no longer my life. I like owning a bed and breakfast, and I'm happy."

He gave a frustrated sigh. "Trace. Don't be a fool. He's —" Don turned back to watch the snow as it covered the tire tracks. "He won't protect you, you'll only end up in more danger. I have the power to keep you safe. I love you. Come back with me." In one swift motion, he unbuckled his seatbelt, flipped up the console, and slid over to me.

He was on my side of the truck. Jack's truck. His rough kiss stinging my lips as I struggled against him.

He brushed his lips across my neck as I fought against him. No. Not this again. At least here he couldn't pin me to the bed. I did have a few new moves that would send him to his side of the truck.

I didn't know how to find Jack on my own. "Don't." I despised the sensation of being powerless, trapped. I hated Don for making me feel this way … again. "Stop it." I struck him as hard as I could in the confined space.

"Hitting me isn't going to change things."

I needed him to concentrate on what we needed to do. "We can't leave Jack out there helpless."

"Do you want to live in this hick-infested town where the most intellectual event is a barn dance? No plays, no concerts, no art galleries, only miles and miles of scrub, sand, and rocks all covered with snow. For what? A man who can't offer you anything more than a second-rate existence. One who'll tire of you and move on." He put a few inches between us. "You're not the kind of woman who can be happy with a small-town sheriff in a backwater town. You need me."

I pushed him back. "Not now." Or ever. "There's something much more important at stake right now ... a man's life." I could almost hear Lacey say the same thing, "he'll get tired of you." Don's face held alarming determination. Why was I so important to him? There were lots of women in D.C., who would be eager to be with him. I fought against his embrace. I knew of only one way to get a straight answer – ask a straight question. I swallowed hard and asked, "Why did you want me?"

My question caught him off guard. He didn't have a glib answer this time. He said, "What?"

"You had to have a reason why you wanted me with you."

"I love you."

"You rarely told me how you felt about me. Tonight... today you've told me you loved me more than all the time we were together. Not even when we had sex, only when you asked me to marry you. So, again, why me?"

He moved back and shoved his hands deep into the pockets of his coat. He was silent as if he were forming the answer he thought I wanted to hear. Leaning against the door, he said, "My mother abandoned me when I was eight. She ran off with a man who didn't want kids." He turned, so he didn't have to look at me. "I spent the rest of my childhood in one foster home after another. When I was ten, I decided I wasn't going to be a product of the system. From then on, I was at the top of my class. When I graduated from high school, I received a scholarship to college. I learned how to use people to make my life easier." He faced me. "It's worked for all these years. When I met you, I thought you'd be another conquest. Another beautiful woman in my bed. After a few months, I decided you'd make the perfect political wife."

I could see the struggle on his face and in the way his shoulders slumped. I knew this was as hard for him to say, as it was for me to hear. I hadn't known anything about his past. Great. Now, I felt sorry for him.

He bowed his head. "I was arrogant. I thought you were naive and

I could get away with anything. Oh, I know you're smart, but you've been sheltered. I know how your father and Stan protected you. I didn't understand how special you were until you were gone." He looked up sharply, "Give me another chance."

This wasn't the Don March I knew. The man beside me was humbled by his own actions. I wouldn't, no, couldn't be part of his life. "I'm not the person you want. I was never happy in your world of parties and politics."

"I need you." He reached out to take my hand.

I didn't know what to say. He had to know I didn't feel the same way. I scowled out at the wall of snow confining me. I needed to say something. "It's after ten, we need to go check on Jane." I was past asking nicely.

»§«

The morning sun still struggled to make its presence known. Overhead a blurry glow brightened a patch in the storm clouds. The windows were dark when we pulled up to the B&B.

In the dining room, the faint light showed us a fallen Christmas tree, and the broken ornaments were scattered everywhere. "No. Jane?" I shouted. "Jane."

Silence flowed down the stairs and wrapped its chilling arms around me like a shroud.

"Jane?" I felt the now all-too-familiar panic reach for me. "Jane?" This time her name came out in a desperate scream.

"She isn't here," Don said.

I stopped at the foot of the steps. "She has to be."

He'd pointed, "There's water on the floor over here." He stepped back and played the beam of his flashlight across the area. Someone came in with snow on their boots."

"It doesn't make sense. Why take Jane? She had nothing to do with what happened last fall."

"Where would she hide something for you to find?" Don asked.

"I don't know." My world was collapsing. The people in it stolen from me like an early frost steals the flowers of summer. I swiped at the tears running down my face. Without these two-important people, how was I going to go on? Jane was the mother I'd always wanted. But Jack was... oh no. "It can't be." My words were swallowed by the raging storm in and around me.

"Get a hold of yourself." Don shot me an irritated glance.

Cold fear swelled in my stomach. I *wanted* to find Jane, but I *needed* to find Jack. I could no longer compartmentalize events. Hurt and fear had slammed the door and locked it.

"Look at me." He tilted my face toward him. "Where would Jane hide something for you?"

I stared at him dumbly as I felt every muscle in my neck and shoulders tighten.

He shook me hard. "Listen to me. Where would she hide something?"

Where? It would be someplace we'd... "Cookies."

"What?" He sounded as if he were sure I'd lost my mind.

"By the cookies we baked today," I pulled free of his grip. "No. Yesterday."

In the kitchen, we found the broken red, green, and gold shards of the ceramic Christmas container mixed with crushed cookies. I stood paralyzed with the reality confronting me. Jack and now Jane ripped away. I wanted the people responsible — I gasped — I wanted them dead.

Don searched through the decorated treats and glass slivers spread on the floor. There was nothing but broken reminders of what the day should have been. The cookies crunched beneath my boots as I bent down and picked up half of a frosted reindeer. The sprinkles were scraped away, and the sweet coating smeared. I held the broken treat in my hand. We should be arranging them on Jane's Christmas plate. The one that lay empty on the center worktable. The ivory platter was rimmed in bright silver with tiny white snowflakes dotted beside the metallic stripe. I set the broken reindeer on the plate as if it were the last morsel of food in the world. I touched the rim of the plate. As I did, it rocked out of balance.

I tilted the platter up and saw the papers underneath.

"Is that it?" He asked

I unfolded the sheet of paper and focused on the words. Jack's name, address, and his cell number. Below his was my information. Hastily scrawled across the bottom was a phone number. No name, only a number. "This only tells us they knew who we were and where to find us," I said. Why did they have our phone numbers? The B&B, yes. Not my cell or Jack's information. I paced into the dining room then back to the entry. "Wait, how did they get Jack's cell number? I thought it was unavailable." When I got a call from him, the display showed only T43-5 on the screen. Not his name, only the odd combination of a letter and numbers. The first time I'd called Jack I'd gotten a recorded message telling me the number was out of service. He'd had to do something special to his phone, so my call would go through.

I stood paralyzed holding the note as the gravity of the situation filtered through my faltering brain. I needed to tell Brad.

"The people who took Trace have Jane," Don said.

I wrenched my attention from the note in my hand to the face of the man beside me. "You're wrong." Please, God, let him be mistaken. "Maybe Jane is at her house or mine." I ran out the back door and across the parking area. All the time knowing we wouldn't find her in either place.

No one answered when I pounded on her door. I made my way to the path leading to Brique House. Here, under the trees, the snow wasn't as deep. The boughs of the evergreens hold the snow until the weight overwhelms them. Then, the branches bend, and the snow slips to the ground with a slap. I fumbled with the key to my front door.

Don reached around, took the key, and put it into the lock.

I pushed open the door and stepped into the entry as the lights burst on. I pulled Jack's cell phone from my pocket. "Service is back."

I dialed Brad. After I told him what we'd found, he was silent for a few seconds. "Read me the number they have down for Jack."

"It's Jack's," I assured him, but I read it to him anyway. "How did they get it?"

"Give me the number at the bottom."

I repeated it to him.

"I'll call you back." He hung up. It was abrupt even for Brad. I figured someone's Christmas Eve was going to be put on hold. Postponed was so much better than destroyed.

"What did he say?" Don asked.

My panic subsided to the point where a semblance of reason had returned. "He said he'd call back." I dialed again.

"Who are you calling now?"

"Jane." I hoped against hope she was somewhere safe.

It rang. I needed something to fall into place. I glanced around. My living room spread out before me, neat and orderly. The furniture wasn't broken. The walls were free of blood stains. I ran my hand over the antique table behind the sofa.

Finally, someone answered. "Who is this?" a man's voice demanded.

"Is Jane there?"

"Yes, we have her."

My turn. "Who is this?" I held my breath.

"The people who are going to make Jack Trace pay."

I reached out for the back of a chair. "Let them go," I ordered.

Don leaned down and pried the phone away from my ear so he could hear.

"The woman knows too much."

Don motioned for me to keep talking as he pulled out his phone.

"What has the sheriff or Jane done to you?"

"He has to pay. We want money." This guy sounded like a sidekick from a bad 'B' movie.

I felt relief flood through me. I'd assumed the bloody message on Jack's wall meant they were going to make him pay with his life. But money I could come up with. The difficulty came with the blood on the note. Someone was injured. I knew it was Jack. "You have the money you took from the sheriff's house." I had no idea how much that was, but I figured a payoff to an informant would be substantial.

"It's not enough. We want more." His words became rushed. "We want five million dollars. Then you can have what's left of him."

What was left of him? What had they done? My flash of breathing room vanished. Again, I struggled to keep my emotions at bay. It wasn't working. What would my dad do? I smiled. He'd be a hard ass. I could play Dad. After a cleansing breath, I took charge of the situation. I stood straight. "I won't pay if either of them is harmed." The strength in my voice surprised me.

I heard a scuffle then a woman's voice came on. "You will pay, or we'll start sending pieces of them to you in five hours," Mrs. Shaw screeched through the phone.

Brad's warning returned to me. "Dangerous — psychotic." The little voice in my head cautioned me to remain calm. "You want five million? Correct?" I pushed my emotions back down and clutched at what was left of my fortitude. If I didn't think about who they had and what they were doing to them, I could do this.

"Yes."

"Okay, we can make this work. First, I want proof of life for both of them. Then we'll talk money. Do we understand each other?" She damn well better.

"We'll call you with instructions." She hung up.

The time on the cell phone read one o'clock. All this running from Spirit Springs to Mullen and out to the Jessen ranch had eaten up the morning. Now I had to figure out how to raise five million dollars before six o'clock tonight.

Don shook his head. "There wasn't enough time to trace it."

My breath came in rapid little gasps as I stood mute looking at the dark phone. Don reached for me, but I stepped away. I mentioned earlier I'm good in bad situations. When they're over, I crash. Desperation remained with me. I didn't have time to collapse.

I knew Don was involved in this somehow. He put out a comforting hand. I grabbed it and pressed my fingernails into the fleshy part of his thumb. I'd never thought my medical training would be put to this use.

"Ouch, damn it, Ensley." He shook his hand to lessen the pain.

"Stop putting your hands on me." What was it with him? I couldn't make it any clearer how I felt. "What are you fifteen? Why do you keep touching me? It isn't helping anything." My voice sounded forceful. "Knock it off."

"I've missed you so much."

"You should have thought about that months ago," I said. "I'm not going through the list again. You know it as well, no, better than I do. Because I'm sure, there is more I haven't heard about." I stopped afraid I'd gone too far. If I had, I was on my own. For all the help Don had been, I figured it wouldn't make much difference if he left.

He turned his back. He stood silently with his head bowed. When he turned, his eyes were closed. I heard him sigh as he opened them and gazed down at his empty hands. "It's unbearable seeing you with Trace. I don't know what to say or do to make you understand how much I regret what I've done. I've never been in this position. I've never been in love before. I know if you come home with me, we can make a family together."

His last word struck me like a fist to the stomach. The man who stood before me was alone. Truly alone. He had no one. I felt the hot trail of tears as they flowed down my face. Don wanted what I'd had all my life, someone to care for him on a deeper level than a partner in bed. Someone who would always be there for him. I'd had my dad and my brother all my life. Now I had Sophie, Jane, and Jack. At least for now. I knew things would change and Jane and Jack would fade from my life. The reality hurt, but I knew it would happen someday.

I could hear the remorse in his voice and see the regret on his face. It was too late. More tears rolled down my cheek. Part of it was pity for him and the rest was for the lives I needed so desperately to save. I'd spent my life blocking out the pain of severed relationships. Broken loves. First, Phillip in med school had proposed thinking I'd be a meal ticket for him and his girlfriend. Then Don had done essentially the same thing. They'd both made me feel as if I were a commodity to be traded for their benefit. Someone valued only as a means to an end and not for who she was.

Jack was different. He hadn't wanted anything from me. I would be a means for wealth, I was sure he had a lot more money than I did. I couldn't further his career ... whatever that was. "Right now two lives are depending on us. We're their only hope. They have to be our priority." Why did I have to keep reminding him of that fact?

He nodded. "What did they say?" He indicated Jack's phone.

"They're crazy." I held up the cell. "They're going to kill them both if I don't give them five million dollars." Time for rational thinking. I fell back into my comfort zone. I organized my options in a form I could deal with — a list. "If I sell everything, cash out all my investments, take out a loan on the B&B, I can come up with the money. It's going to take time. Time, I don't have." I put some distance between Don and me.

"You're going to sell everything? You..." His expression turned cruel and hard. "Did they say if they had the money, I gave Trace?" His tone sounded calculating.

I watched him as I said, "Yes. They want more than the money you had for the exchange. I can't get it in the time they've given me."

Don crossed his arms, "The government has a policy, no money for hostages."

Was this it? Was this the way I'd lose Jack? To a bunch of crazed criminals?

Chapter Nine

"We need to stall them," Don was saying. "Tell them you have to wait for the banks to open on the twenty-sixth,"

"First, I am not leaving them in the hands of those people. Brad said they were crazy and worse, sadistic. Second, I don't think they'll wait." My shoulder muscles had cramped into hard knots.

He began to pace. "There are two factions. One wants revenge on Trace, the other wants money. For now, the money people have held off the killers. It won't last long."

"That's the reason we can't wait," I said. There *was* a division. I'd heard it when Mrs. Shaw had wrestled the phone from the man who'd answered it. I knew the first voice wasn't Mr. Shaw. These people were working at cross purposes. "Who are they?"

Don stopped pacing. "One is local," he muttered. "That has to be it. My intel was right," He paused. "But why is he —?" Then as if he remembered I was there, he stopped.

"You know who's behind this." When he didn't appear to hear me, I shoved him. "Tell me what's going on."

He ignored me. "With the electricity on. We can call CSU and see what they've found."

I lifted Jack's cell phone and stared at it. I could almost see it blink

You're running out of time. I had five hours to get the money and sort out what was really going on. I had to find them.

I didn't know the CSU number. We were wasting time. Wait. The number at the bottom of the piece of paper we'd found. "Where's the paper Jane hid for me?"

His hand went to his coat pocket. "Why?"

"We need to call the number at the bottom of the note. If we're facing two groups, the number must be the other group," I pointed out.

"No. We don't want to tip our hand. When we get them both back, we'll call it." He watched me from across the entry. "I've been through this a hundred times. You've got to understand the odds of us finding them alive are slim. In all probability, they're already dead."

"I can't." I studied his face. "I will not lose them. I've already lost so much."

His eyes were the color of ice. Deep, pitiless, ice. "I'll do what I can." There was something behind his words. What had he left unsaid? Whatever it was, I knew it was significant. Did he know more than he'd let on? Of course, he always did. In D.C., I'd found it unsettling. No matter what I told him, he was never surprised. It was as if he already knew. It bothered me to the point I'd searched my office and house for listening devices. In the end, I dismissed the impressions as an overactive imagination. It wasn't the first time my crazy side had escaped.

I called Phyllis and asked for CSU's number.

"I called there the minute the power came back on," she said. "No one answered. It must still be out in Mullen,"

I thanked her and told Don what she'd said.

"Let's go see what the lab rats have for us."

I blinked. Lab rats. What a total jerk. Did Don think of me like that? No. He'd never been interested in my professional life. Until he destroyed it. I'd been more of a garnishment, like the parsley on his dinner plate. No real worth just there to be decorative. I shook off the lousy feeling. He understood it took a special woman to be a wife in the spotlight. They're made of a lot sterner stuff than people know. You've seen the wives of men in the public eye stand behind them as they confessed to some indiscretion. He's finally figured out I was that strong woman. Too bad, he hadn't figured out I wouldn't be that woman for him.

Time raced toward the deadline. I had to try to get the cash they wanted. Why hadn't I thought of this before? Uncle Stan. He'd know what to do. I pulled out Jack's phone and called him.

"Hello?"

"Uncle Stan, it's Ensley."

"Pumpkin, how can I help?"

"You know what's going on?" I asked.

"Brad Hughes called me," he cleared his throat. "Have you found out anything new?" I had to break the news to him about Jane. I steeled myself and said, "Uncle Stan, they have Jane too."

"God, no. Not Janie."

Silence.

I told him about the ransom demand. "I can't get the money in time."

"Even if you could, it wouldn't do any good. Jack is the best at what he does. If he can, he'll get the two of them out of this." He gave a long deep sigh. "If he can't — I'm worried about both of them."

"I'm not going to stand by and let them die. I have too much at stake."

"Ensley, I do not want you doing something stu — you're not prepared to do. Are we clear?"

Whoops, Ensley. He only called me by my given name when he was upset with me. "I'll be okay. Don March is —"

"Let me speak to him."

This was not going to end well.

I held out the phone. "Stan Hofstadter wants to talk to you." For a second he looked at the device as if he wasn't sure what it was.

"Great." He took the phone. "General, I'm doing everything I can — No one can get in or out. I'm counting on the storm lasting long enough for me — I'm aware of who he is — no I'm not going to jeopardize their lives. — I resent the implication." He stopped and looked down at me. "Don't threaten me." He closed his eyes in frustration.

"I'll do everything I can." Without another word, he shoved the phone at me.

"Pumpkin, I don't know what March is up to, but you can be sure," he paused. "I've got some calls to make."

"Uncle Stan," I had one more question. "Have you found out about the phone number I gave to Brad?" I had to know who was on the other end of that number.

"Pumpkin." The silence that traveled between us was more frightening than any answer he could have given me.

"They're terrorists, aren't they?"

"Brad is still tracing it. Listen to me. There is someone there besides the Shaw's. You take care. Do you hear me? Whatever you do, don't go out there."

"Who else is out there?"

"Right now, it's only speculation. When we know for sure, I'll let you know. I can't say this enough. Do not go out there."

"I've got to get them back." It was all I could manage.

"Don't do anything until we can get there, it's too dangerous. I mean it, Ensley."

There was nothing else to be said. I couldn't find Jack alone. Uncle Stan, and Brad couldn't get here, and whoever was coming from the Boise side wouldn't be here either.

I followed Don back through the trees.

When we reached the parking lot by the B&B, I saw Jack's truck. For a flash, I thought he was back. Safe. A micro-second later, reality crashed down on me. Stay steady. Stay steady. I repeated over and over in my head. This is who I am. The girl who's always steadfast, the one able to deal with whatever is thrown at her. The one who's not used to relying on anyone else.

This time was different. On top of everything else, it came too close on the heels of the trauma of last fall. I'd fought back toward normal with the help of Jane, but I knew I couldn't have done it without Jack. He'd been there every time I needed him. No pressure, only the gentle touch of his hand and the strength in his voice.

The pain brought with it the realization that the two people who'd helped me along the way were now counting on me to save them. On some level — not the one that puts things into solid words, but in the very essence of my heart — I knew if I failed today my future would be lost to me.

»§«

At two o'clock, Luke opened the CSU lab door for us. "I'm glad you're here. I have something for you."

We walked along an ordinary corridor of mundane-colored tile that lead to a beige door and, behind it, a hospital green lab. The walls were painted concrete block. Butted up against them were nondescript tables, no personal pictures or Christmas decorations in sight. The only spot of color was a periodic table of elements hanging on the far wall. At least that was in color.

Luke plucked a slide from the table. "This tells us where they are or at least, where they've been. I'd bet on it."

"What is it?" Don took the slide.

"Motor oil."

"*That* narrows it down to almost everywhere." Don's sarcastic tone wasn't lost on either of us. "Gas stations, truck stops, garages, homes where they change their own oil. I assume people around here do that sort of thing. Should I keep going?"

Luke shook his head. "Not this. It's the new synthetic stuff. No one around here uses it much. It's expensive. Only one place here in Mullen even carries it."

"He may have walked through it." Don handed back the slide.

"If he did, he had to splash through a puddle of it. It was on his shoes and pant legs."

"Maybe he's a mechanic," I said. I held fast to this new thread of hope. It would narrow our list of suspects.

"Jimmy, the guy at the motel, is a car nut. If this guy worked in a garage, Jimmy would know him."

I turned to Don. "He lied to us."

"I *do not* like being lied to." Don shifted his attention to Luke. "Where does this Jimmy live?"

"No idea." Luke reached for his phone. "Maybe my sister does."

He dialed. "Hey, you remember Jimmy, the guy you went out with a few months back? Yeah, the car guy. Where's he live?" He waited. "Thanks. Tell Mom I'll be over when I can. Bye." To us, he said, "He still lives with his mother." He wrote down the address and handed it to me.

"Figures," Don took the slip of paper.

"Thanks, Luke," I said. "And thanks for everything. You should go home to your family." I hoped we wouldn't need him again.

With Jimmy's mother's address in hand, we drove across town to a neighborhood drowned in snow. The plows hadn't made it out here. In all our travels, I hadn't seen any sign of them anywhere. Maybe they were waiting for a break in the winter onslaught.

I looked out at the house across the street. "What now?" The snow drifts were getting deeper. Everything was covered in almost three feet of new snow. "Do we walk up, knock on the door, and ask her if her son is a kidnapper?"

"That's not very subtle. Let's try a less obvious approach."

"I don't have any subtle left. I do have a lot of blatant. I want someone's butt on a platter."

"I've never seen you like this. What happened to my calm, rational girl?" He frowned. "The one I asked to marry me?"

"I left her up on a snow-covered mountain —" I pointed toward the failed ski resort, "while I was fighting for my life and Jack's. Events and this town have changed me."

"Trace again." He reached for the truck's door handle. "Let's get this over with."

I caught up with him as he crossed the street. "This isn't the kind of place you'd hold someone, two someone's, hostage. We're in a small town in the country, not in the impersonal city. People here know their neighbors." Of course. "They aren't being held in either Mullen or Spirit Springs." I snapped my fingers, which didn't make any noise because of my mittens. "They have to be in a secluded place. It must be a ranch they can get to. The Jessen's ranch."

"We were out there. We'd have seen some signs."

Any clue we may have found was now covered in more snow.

I wasn't wrong. I knew how information traveled through Spirit

Springs. I figured it was the same in Mullen. I took in the street around us. The post-World War II houses were all decorated. All except the one we were walking toward. Around us, the falling snow distorted the holiday lights.

Someone had cleared the sidewalks. They'd probably gotten a brand-new snow blower for Christmas and opened it early out of necessity. In the house next door to our target, a Santa form stuck out of a snowdrift. The only parts still visible were the top of his head and the fingers on his waving hand. His eight-tiny reindeer were buried up to their antlers.

"Don't you see? It makes sense. If Brad is right —" And I knew he was — "Jessen's daughter would have access to his ranch."

"No one even knew about her, which tells me she hasn't been around. She wasn't part of his life. You can't step back into a person's life and expect to be..." His words had a personal ring to them. I knew now all his ambition was because he was trying to prove himself. Impress a mother who'd never been around and never would be. Despite everything, a flood of compassion surged through me.

In all the months we'd been together, tonight was the first time he'd ever mentioned his family and then only his mother. It must have been painful for him when I rambled on about Cole and my dad. Of course, my attachment to Sophie, mama, papa and the boys — my other family. Being around them had to be salt in his wound. I had people who held me as close as if I were one of them. "Don." What? I'm sorry?

For an instant, I saw a different Don March. Not the hard CIA agent, but a sad little boy. A lost frightened child.

"The point is," he cleared his throat. "A child doesn't accept an absent parent as if all is forgiven. As if, their absence didn't matter." I'd seen him in a lot of situations. I'd never seen him struggle this way. For the first time since I'd known him, his expression turned vulnerable. As fast as it had appeared, it vanished, and he resumed his mask of a self-confidence CIA supervisor. "The point is," he said, "a child doesn't accept an absent parent as if all is forgiven. As if, their absence didn't matter."

"Maybe. The thing is, she cared enough about her father to

threaten Jack and me last fall and to put together a group to kidnap Jack and Jane now." He may know a lot about the crime part of this situation, but I knew something he didn't. A special bond exists between fathers and daughters.

"He didn't acknowledge her. That had to affect her," he said as he turned toward the house.

"If she didn't care, why go to all this trouble? She lost two of her group taking Jack."

He gazed down at me as if I were a stupid child. "She wants money. People like her don't care about the casualties. Trace never did. Let's get this over with."

Why did he hate Jack with so much passion?

"Does it ever quit snowing here?" Don snapped.

"Nobody's home," called a woman walking her dog. At least, I assumed she was. She held one of those retractable leashes in her hand. The dog wasn't tall enough to be seen over the mound of snow in front of her. "Haven't been for a while." Her red puffy jacket and short gray hair peeking out from under a red knit hat gave her a Mrs. Claus look. The only thing missing was a pair of wire-rimmed glasses and a plate of cookies.

I left Don and waded back to her. "Do you know where they went?"

"Bonnie won a trip south." She adjusted her scarf up around her neck. "I wish I was in a warmer climate. My joints ache." She paused. "Good luck for her. Still, it was odd."

"Why is it odd?" Don asked over my shoulder.

She tilted her head as a puzzled look showed on her face. "It's Christmas. She's been gone for a few days. Not due back until Monday next." She looked from Don to me. "I'd want to be with my family this time of year."

Yeah, me too. "How about Jimmy?" I tried to make it sound as if we knew the family. "Is he around?"

"He only comes by when he wants something. Usually money. Bonnie spoiled the boy something awful. He turned out selfish and mean."

"I take it you don't care for him," Don said.

"No-good kid. First, he was going to be a mechanic. I let him change the oil in my lawnmower. He tore it all apart. When he couldn't fix it, he took it to the dealer downtown and had the repairs charged to me. A new one would have been cheaper. Then, he was going to be an accountant. It must have required effort because he's working at the motel down by the highway."

"I'm Don March." He offered her his hand.

"Gertrude Goode." She grinned up at him.

"Have you seen him around lately, Gertrude?" Don chatted with her like she was his favorite neighbor.

"He was here this morning. You only missed him by a couple of hours or so." She smiled at Don as her little dog began to whine. She reached down and picked up the mini-pooch.

From her expression, I guessed he was smiling back. He had a charming smile when he wanted. His smooth manner lured people into telling him anything he wanted. Something he usually ended up using to his advantage. I'd fallen for his enticements more than once.

"Did you talk to him?" Don asked.

She took a step closer to him. "Yes. He was in a hurry. I wished him a Merry Christmas. He said something about it being the best ever. Struck me as off since his mother was gone."

"Did he mention where he was going?"

She gave Don another smile. "No. Just hopped in his little truck and left." She laughed. "It's a piece of junk. He's probably stuck somewhere."

"Do you know where he lives now?" I asked.

Her little dog was shivering. "He got a place over to the new apartments east of town. Valley View Village, I think it's called." She hugged her dog to her. "I've got to get Sparkle inside before she freezes."

"You've been very helpful." Don removed a card from his pocket. "If you think of anything else, or he comes back." He wrote his cell number on the card. "Please, give me a call."

She took the card. "Oh. CIA. I sure will."

"I'd appreciate it if you'd keep this between us."

Her eyes grew wide with excitement as if 007 himself was asking her to keep a vital secret for queen and country. "I will. My Frank was in the Navy. You can count on me." She watched as we got into Jack's truck.

Don waved to her as we left.

"You're very smooth," I said.

"I used to be in the field, remember?" He paused. "We need to talk."

"Oh, no. Not again. What's the point? We never get anything settled." I'd had all the talk I wanted from him. There wasn't anything more to be said. I knew how he felt. He knew how I felt. Nothing would change with more words. No matter how many times he said, we needed to talk. The problem was every time he started the conversation, I ended up with him a whole lot closer than I wanted.

Wait, if he wanted to chat, we would. This time, it was going to be on my terms. I had only one question. "Why did you really come here?" I held up my hand as he started to protest. "I know what you said, but I want the real reason. Anyone of your men could make this exchange. Why Jack? Why now?" Okay, maybe I had a few more questions. "You said you couldn't stand seeing me with Jack but, you haven't truly seen me with him. I know you were the one who wanted me at the bar and grill. Why? Those few minutes were all you saw of us together." I remembered thinking he had a listening device in my office or my house in D.C. Now it appeared he had someone sending him information from Spirit Springs. If he did, it answered so many questions. One last question. "Why did Jack agree to have me at the bar and grill?"

He stared at me silently. Finally, he started the truck. "I'll tell you when this is all over."

In the stillness, I wondered why he hadn't had a sharp comeback. I wanted a reasonable explanation, one I was sure, I'd never get. It didn't matter anymore. My here and now was closing in around me. I had more important things to worry about.

Don pulled to a stop at the Winston Motel.

"Why are we here?"

"I want to talk to Jimmy's boss."

"It's Christmas Eve. He's at home, with his family." I hadn't meant it to sound like I was talking to a stupid child, but it did.

He sized up the situation. "Then, we go to his house."

The snow-clouds hung heavy and dark above us. Only a miserable amount of sun made the journey through the snow-filled clouds as the day slipped away. "We only have only four hours left."

"They want the money more than anything," Don said.

He didn't know that, and besides, "I don't have it."

Jack's cell rang.

"We got another rock through the window." It was Phyllis. "What is it with these people? They have our phone number. "This one is covered with blood, too," her voice came out in a strained whisper as if her nerves were shredded. "I don't like this. I want my sheriff back."

So did I. "It has to be the proof of life we wanted. We'll be right there." I pushed end.

"Where?"

"Another rock through the Sheriff's Office window."

The dashboard clock screamed the time. Three-thirty. They'd had Jack for fourteen hours.

Chapter Ten

"Ensley, over here," Phyllis said. "I got through to CSU and Luke is on his way. He said we shouldn't touch it until he gets here."

Lois watched me but, she remained near the stone as if guarding it. It must smell like Jack.

"Is that kid, Luke, the most senior person at the lab?" Don asked.

"He is for now. Everyone else is on vacation," Phyllis said.

"I want the person in charge. Call them back."

"There's no point." Phyllis folded her arms and leveled her gaze at him. "The head of the lab went to his folks in Boise for Christmas. Even if he wanted to he's not going to make it back in this storm."

"Find someone who can," Don said.

"I'll call the sheriff in Mullen," I said as I reached for the office phone.

"No. I don't want some hick sheriff over here bungling things."

Phyllis and I exchanged annoyed glances.

Don's cell rang. He took it out as he walked into Jack's office.

"I don't like him." Phyllis watched Don. "Oh, I'm sorry. You used to be engaged." She stole another glance at Don. "You're better off with Jack. Much better off."

I slumped against her desk and glanced at Lois and the rock. *If he's still alive.* The thought had my heart punching hard at my ribs. "How did you find out about Don and me?"

"Jane. We talked earlier. She's worried about you and Jack. I don't mind telling you, I do not like people stealing my sheriff."

"Phyllis, why don't you go home?"

"Someone has to staff the office." She averted her eyes. "I don't like some CIA agent in here thinking he knows more than we do." She was aiming her anger and frustration at the most convenient solid object she could, Don.

I focused on the issue at hand. "When did Luke say he'd be here?"

"Now," Luke said from the door as he and Carl entered. "I'm sorry it's taking so long, but the snow is slowing everything down to a crawl. I just hope it doesn't take out the power lines again." He shook the snow from his coat and hat. "Where's the new rock?"

Both men snapped on latex gloves. Luke bent down and picked it up off the floor. Lois followed him to the desk. "I wish we had the facilities to check DNA." Lois followed him to the desk. "I'd like to know who all this blood belongs to."

Lois and I knew.

I watched him meticulously inspect the rock and the paper attached to it. I could feel the seconds ticking away. Each one screaming at me to hurry. My time was running out. I had to get the money. But how? Jack's cell rang.

"Hello."

"Ensley, Brad. The number you gave me is troubling."

Curiosity had me wondering how a phone number could be *troubling.* "Why?"

"It comes back to a burner. The problem came when I called it." He paused then said, "Let me talk to March."

I could *almost* see the puzzle pieces fitting together. They were right in front of me, but I needed them down on paper to see how they meshed.

I went into Jack's office and handed the phone to Don. "It's Brad. He wants to talk to you."

"I'll call you later," Don told the person on his phone. "March," he said into Jack's phone. "How —" He covered the phone and said to me. "Would you check on the CSU technicians?"

I didn't want to leave, but I figured whatever they were going to talk about was classified. Out in the main room, Luke was unwrapping the note from the stone. After removing the letter, he smoothed it out. It was torn in a couple of places from its trip through the window.

"That's not what I asked for. Where's our proof of life?" I stared at the bloody note. If this was meant to terrorize us. It was working.

"What's it say?" Don asked as he joined us.

"Five million." Luke flipped it over. "Nothing else. No message."

I called Jane's phone. They picked it up on the first ring.

"You got the demand?" a man said.

"This isn't what we agreed on. Where's my proof of life? No proof. No money."

"Do you have —?"

After a scuffle, Mrs. Shaw came on. "Do you have the money?"

"What I don't have is proof of life. Wasn't I clear earlier? No proof. No money. How much more concise can I make it?"

"I'll kill them both."

"Here's the deal. I need more time. The money is on the way, but it's going to be a while because of the holidays and the snow. More important, if I don't get proof of life, there won't be any money. If you kill them, I *will* hunt you down, and I *will* end you. Each and every one of you. I'll have nothing left to lose. Now, do we understand each other?"

"I want my money."

"And I *want* my people. So, we do understand each other."

"We'll be in touch." The line went dead.

Through my tears the red end bar was a blur. Even if I'd been able to see it, I was shaking so hard I would have missed the phone entirely. I don't know who hung it up.

I wiped my eyes and glanced at the four faces staring at me, three were stunned, and one was angry.

"And I thought the sheriff was tough," Luke said. "I'll get you a copy of this." He put his hand on my shoulder. "You'll find them," he whispered as he passed me.

I'd prepared for this. I knew what the worst-case scenario was. I tried to breathe. My future was out in the snow-covered desert. I hoped I wouldn't have to figure out how to survive their deaths. "It was my turn to be the bully," was all I could say.

Phyllis hugged me. "You're going to be fine," she whispered. "We're stronger than they know." She motioned toward the men.

I wasn't so sure.

Without a word, Don walked back into Jack's office.

I grabbed a tablet from the desk and a pen, and sat down, Lois came over. I sank to the floor. She cuddled into me. I remembered the first time I'd met her. It was the night my dad died. She'd been the welcoming committee when I'd arrived at Jack's. Her very presence then was as therapeutic as it was now. "I'm going to make this right," I promised her, all the while knowing it was going to take a miracle. A Christmas miracle. I scanned the red and green decorations littering the office.

If I was going to figure this out, I needed to see it in writing.

The first thing I put down was:

How had they been able to take Jack at his house, on his turf. That still puzzled me. Jack is too smart and too skilled to be taken by people like the Shaw's.

There had to be someone else there. Could it be the people on the other end of that mysterious phone number? Whoever the person was they had to be as skilled as Jack.

How did the terrorist angle fit in? If they were involved how did they get tangled up with the Shaws?

Where were they? They couldn't be far. No one was getting in or out of the valley. I decided that was a good-news-bad-news situation. Everything now seemed to have that component to it.

The last rock through the window had an ominous feel to it. No it had more of a psychological component. Meant only to frighten.

The Shaws were mean and crazy, but the other faction was a lot more chilling. Everything *circled around to the mystery person or people.* I felt they were all tangled up with Don and his mission here. Whatever that was.

I laid my pen and paper on the floor beside me and rubbed Lois's soft ears. She opened her eyes, eyes that held all the sadness I felt. This wasn't the Christmas I'd expected. Oh, I knew it was going to be hard without my dad. Not in my wildest imagination did I expect to be sitting alone on the floor of the Sheriff's Office, clinging to Lois and desperate to find two people I cared deeply for. Both depending on me to save their lives.

Mentally drained, I gleaned every ounce of comfort I could from my furry companion. She laid her head back down on my lap. I closed my eyes and ran my fingers along Lois's velvet-soft ears. Her even breathing brought with it calm. I concentrated on the rhythmic rising and falling of her chest and nothing else.

"Ensley, I think I have something." Luke knelt next to us.

I blinked up at him. "What is it?" Gently, I lifted Lois's head. She popped right up.

"I checked this rock for the synthetic oil. It's on this one, too." He looked down at the floor. "I should have checked the other one first thing. I'm sorry."

"You're doing great. I'm impressed you found it at all." Since I didn't know what the oil meant, I asked.

"I think it's from the Jessen ranch. They bought a couple new ATV's before all that happened last fall. They were the ones they used up in the hills when they were after you and the Sheriff. It's hard to believe Max Jessen was out to kill you both. I guess people do all kinds of things for money." He cleared his throat. "Anyway, Max bragged about the ATV's to everyone. He said he'd only use the new synthetic oil because they were high performance." He paused. "I didn't think about it before because no one's out there."

"Oil?" I was exhausted to the point my cognitive processes were lagging far behind what I needed them to be. "I should have remembered. There was a case of oil broken in one of the sheds at the Jessen ranch when we were there earlier." I got up from the floor. "Did you tell Don?"

Luke shook his head. "He's been sitting in the sheriff's office. He was talking on the phone. Since he hung up, he's been staring at something on the wall."

"Thanks. I'll tell him." If Luke was right, they *were* at the Jessen ranch. But where? I walked to Jack's office. "Don?"

He swiveled around. His face was emotionless. "Yes."

"Luke found the same oil on the rock that he found on the dead man's shoes. Do you remember the broken case of oil we found in the old building at the Jessen place?"

"The building was filthy. There was garbage everywhere."

"Pay attention. Remember the case that had fallen over? I didn't think much of it at the time, but I'm sure it was oil. That must be where the dead man at Jack's got it on his pants. Luke found it on both rocks. It has to be where they are."

"The oil is probably in a dozen different places."

"Listen to me. With more than three feet of new snow on the ground," I pointed outside, "they'd have to have a place where there's bare ground. They aren't going to dig through all this snow for rocks."

"We need to wait here for their call."

"Then what? We can't fake five million dollars." I took in the wall he'd been staring at when I came in. It was full of pictures of Jack's Army buddies and certificates. I'd seen them all, dozens of times.

"Know who they are?" Don sat forward. "Jack's last team."

Ten smiling faces mugged for the camera.

"Want to know what happened to them?"

"Not now." I had enough to think about, and we had to get to the Jessen ranch.

He acted as if he hadn't heard me. "A week after this photo was taken half of them were dead."

One more dagger of sadness stabbed my heart. I took a step forward to get a better look. Jack knelt in front with two other men. A black man with a cheesy grin and a red-haired man who was laughing.

"Want to know how they died?" He motioned to the wall.

"No." I didn't want to hear Don's version of anything to do with Jack.

"You should know what kind of man he is before you give up everything for him."

I shot him my best annoyed look.

"Later."

This was classic Don March. "I don't have time for your head games. Either tell me or not." I wasn't going to let him have any more control than he already had.

"If I had the backup, I'd take them out," Don said.

"That would put Jack and Jane in more danger. It's not an option."

"It doesn't matter. We don't know where they are."

Wasn't he listening? "I just told you they were at the Jessen ranch."

"We were there. The place was abandoned."

"Because we didn't check all the buildings." Remember Mr. Smart-guy?

"I don't have the manpower to go after them."

"You have Oliver, Lyle and me." I was too exhausted to remember the rest of the officers' names.

"You're not going. I'm not taking the others, they aren't trained."

"Lyle is a former Army Scout. He just got out of the service a few months ago. I don't know about Oliver. No matter what, you aren't leaving me behind. Jack and Jane are going to need medical attention." I took a step toward the door. "I've gotten pretty good at patching holes in people."

He got up and walked out into the main room. "Phyllis, what training does Oliver have?"

"He's been on the force for six years."

"Military. What's his military training?"

"He's in the reserves."

"They'll do. Get them in here." He might as well have been barking orders at a private.

She raised one eyebrow and crossed her arms. "If you say please."

"Fine. Please."

She picked up the phone and called the men.

I thought it vital to point out; "We now know they're at the Jessen ranch, we still don't know in which building. We can't go blundering around. They'll see us."

"The Army Scout, what's his name? Lyle? Should be able to get in, pinpoint them and get out without being seen. If we're lucky, we'll get them back and live to tell about it." He reached for me then stopped. He must have finally gotten the idea I wasn't going back to him. "Then we're going to sit down and have a long talk. I'm going to tell you everything." His words sounded more like a threat than a promise.

Jack's cell phone rang.

"Is this the doctor?" It was Mrs. Shaw.

"Yes."

"We have a problem."

Chapter Eleven

Dread swamped my brain cells, as the muscles in my neck twisted into a Gordian knot. "What kind of problem?" The strength in my voice was all for show. I leaned hard against the desk.

"One of my men got a little carried away. Your friend isn't going to make it if you don't get here fast."

My heart slammed against my chest as my breath caught in my throat. "What've you done?" I swallowed hard. "Where are you?"

"I'm not going to tell you, you'll tell the police."

I pulled myself together. "Then how in the hell am I supposed to find you?" The command in my voice matched my rigid stance.

"Go to the Gas and Gulp. The cashier will have instructions. Don't bring anyone and leave your cell phone behind. And don't forget the money."

I didn't look at Don. "I'm on my way." The line went dead.

I walked back into the main room. I didn't want to be in Jack's office with Don one more second.

I dialed Brad. "We have a problem. The kidnappers called, and one of the hostages is severely injured."

"I'm still in Salt Lake. Do not. I repeat, *do not* go to the kidnappers." He cleared his throat. "Ensley. You can't do this."

"I can't live with any other choice."

"Damn it. I wish you wouldn't." A longer pause. "Jack has a way of getting through the most impossible situations." His lull held a silent sigh. "That was when he didn't have anyone to come home to."

I didn't know how to process his words. "Wish me luck." We hung up.

Don stood in my way. "You're not going anywhere."

"Oh, really. I don't see anyone here who can stop me."

"I'll lock you in a jail cell if I have to."

"Seriously?" It wouldn't stop me. "I'm going." I shoved my way past him.

He took hold of my arm, again. "You don't have any idea what he is, or what these people are capable of." His grip tightened until my arm hurt. "Ensley, you don't know who's out there."

"But you do, don't you?" At that moment, I wanted to make him feel the way I did. I stared into his eyes. The eyes I'd once gazed into as we made love. The same ones that had shown real emotion when he'd told me of his childhood. I knew he already hurt as much as he could. It was the kind of pain that lives deep inside you. One you can never sooth. "I won't abandon them to die out there alone."

His eyes became colder than the temperature outside.

"What aren't you telling me? You have something to do with this, don't you?" I wanted to rip his throat out. My breathing increased.

"You're coming with me." He pulled me into Jack's office and shut the door hard enough to rattle the glass. "You need to hear the story. Why he's in this town."

"Not now. I —" I had to get to Jack and Jane.

"No. Now. Before you risk your life for a man, who's an imposter. He isn't who you think he is. Before you give up everything for a murderer." Don stood with his hand holding the door shut. "I sent Trace on a mission to Africa. To rescue plane crash victims. The daughter of a high-ranking diplomat was on board. A terrorist group captured the passengers. Trace and his team went in posing as expats, go-betweens in an off-the-record ransom exchange." He sounded like he was giving a briefing. No emotion. "They took a sack of diamonds to swap for the girl. When they arrived, they found not only the daughter but everyone who'd been on the plane with her. There were thirty people in all. The drug lord wanted more money. Trace gambled and seduced the leader's daughter, hoping to get her to convince her father to give them more time. With that time, he thought he'd be able to get everyone out. He was — is good with women." His eyes narrowed as he watched me.

His words from earlier echoed in my head. "And you fell for it." I raised my chin and met his gaze.

"Your father and Stan Hofstadter were in theater," he continued. "The situation was a powder keg. All those girls, the diplomat's daughter, the crew of the plane." He shook his head. "One wrong move and they'd all die. Everything hinged on Trace's influence over the headman's daughter. Then, it went sideways. All hell was about to rain down. It would have made Blackhawk Down, and Benghazi look like church picnics. None of them were going to make it out. Casualties of war. A public relations nightmare. It wasn't my problem."

I suppressed the overwhelming urge to slap him. A public relations nightmare? They were people. Soldiers and civilians who were in desperate need of Don's help.

"Your father and Hofstadter were ordered to stand down and wait for negotiations to proceed. The drug lord's daughter discovered Trace had used her. When she told her father, he sent every man he had after Trace, his team and the others. As payback, Trace murdered the woman he'd slept with."

He watched me as if I was a virus under a microscope. "When Trace finally radioed for extraction, it was too late. We couldn't chance putting helicopters in there. Your father and Hofstadter disobeyed direct orders. I don't know how they did it, but they got troops in there. Trace made it out with everyone on the plane, but with only half his men. That picture," he pointed to the photo of smiling faces, "was taken a week before the mission. To make matters worse, the ransomed diamonds disappeared along with millions of dollars in drug money. Your father and Hofstadter were allowed to retire. Trace, of course, came out of it with a couple of medals," Don nearly spit out the last sentence. "And it would appear millions." He paused. "How do you think he can afford that house?"

Jack sounded as ruthless as Don. I reminded myself who was telling the story. Still, I felt my heart break a little.

"After the failed mission, Trace moved out here three years ago. First thing he did was build his million-dollar house. You pretty much know the rest. Have you asked Lacey, the bartender, why she keeps going after him?" He considered me for a few seconds. "I did. They used to be lovers until you came along. It's how he operates. When the next one enters the picture, you'll end up like sad little Lacey. Wondering what happened. Hoping he'll come back when he gets tired of his new prize."

"I don't believe you." My sympathy for him vanished.

Don smiled. "See how good he is? He knew you'd say that."

He had. I'd heard him in the bar say, "She won't believe you." "This is what I'm going to do." I didn't keep my voice down the way he had. "I'll get the two of them back. Then, I'll deal with the rest of it." I pounded my fist hard into the center of his chest, "After that I'll deal with you. Now, get the hell out of my way. I shoved him aside. I wasn't sure my shaky knees would carry me out the door. I stopped, turned and demanded, "Give me the keys to Jack's truck."

I passed an opened-mouthed Phyllis. I wanted desperately to stop and ask her about Lacey. Ask her if Jack was as ruthless as Don said he was. I couldn't. I was afraid of her answer.

»§«

I slid behind the wheel of the large Ford truck. I was crying, again. "Damn it." Tears blurred my vision as I pulled into the parking lot of the Gas and Gulp. I didn't know what I'd find. Half of me was afraid this was a trap; the other half was just plain terrified. My hand shook as I reached for the door handle. I can deal with change, I'm not afraid of it. I've dealt with it all my life. This was one change I didn't know if I could handle.

Don's story had shaken me to my very core. To the very heart of me.

Dad. Uncle Stan. Had they… was it true? I'd always thought Dad's money had come from wise stock choices, good investments. Had they all shared in the drug money and diamonds? No. It wasn't… it couldn't be true. I was going to hold tight to what I'd known all these years. I wasn't going to believe anything Don said. I sure wasn't going to be his *prize*.

Jack told me he inherited his money from his grandmother. I'd straighten this out when I got Jack and Jane home. "Compartmentalize," I said out loud. If I didn't, none of us would survive. The problem was the emotional compartment in my head was full.

I ran my hand over the leather of the seat in Jack's new truck. Was this short chapter in my life ending? The sense of belonging, of being — I refused to let the last word form in my head. I hadn't been here long enough. Yet I knew. I knew he was the only man I'd ever loved. Why couldn't I fall for a nice safe scientist? Or a banker?

I stepped out into the storm. It rivaled the one raging inside me. I shivered more from my emotions than the blizzard.

The parking lot sat empty. The cars and semis had taken their people home for the holiday. The twenty-foot light poles over the gas pumps were bright in the early evening gloom. A billboard at the end of the lot blinked red and green as it enticed travelers in to buy gas at the lowest price in fifty miles and wished them a Merry Christmas. At some point, a plow had scraped the new snow to the far end of the lot. By the size of the pile, it would still be melting in June. Would I be here to see it melt? It didn't look like it.

I walked up to the store entrance.

Someone had scratched their initials in the bright green holly painted on the glass door. I pushed it open. The only person inside was a bored-looking woman slouched behind the cash register watching *It's a Wonderful Life*. "Hello, this is going to sound odd, but did someone leave something here for Ensley Markus?"

She glanced up. "You the doctor?"

"Yes."

"Then, yeah." She slid an envelope across the counter to me. At least, it wasn't covered with blood.

"Thank you." I touched it as if it might blow up. Why not? Metaphorically, everything else in my life had in the last eighteen hours.

"You going to buy something?"

"What?"

"You want something?" Her gum snapped with her last word.

"Something?" I repeated dumbly. "Yes. Water." I went to the refrigerated case and chose two of the largest bottles they had. People don't think about drinking water in the winter, but it's just as important when it's cold. I figured the kidnappers wouldn't have shared any with Jack or Jane.

Back in the truck, I opened the envelope. "Go to the Jessen Ranch. Drive around behind the new house. Take the road to the end." That was it, nothing more. The back of the paper was blank. Had they been at the ranch all along? Could this have all been over hours ago if we'd searched the whole place? I started the Ford. If only I'd insisted, no, demanded we search farther. Still, there had been no other obvious buildings, or road. Why hadn't I been more forceful instead of acquiescing to Don's expertise?

I steered out onto the highway. I wasn't sure which was churning more. My head, my stomach, or my heart, or the raging storm. I knew Don would do anything to get what he wanted. Now, it appeared, so would Jack. I remembered Lacey's words. "He'll get tired of you and come back to me." Oh, God, was it all true? Was Jack that skillful?

I remembered when we were in the mountains. He'd told me to stay behind the tractor. Not to come out unless he came back. Had it been an act? Had he known the FBI was there all along? Then there was the fact I hadn't been able to find out much about his past. All he'd tell me was he'd been raised by his grandmother. It appeared the rest of the people in Spirit Springs had no idea who they'd elected sheriff.

A massive semi-truck screamed past me, churning up snow and causing a whiteout. I slowed.

If Jack had done everything Don said he had, I wasn't going to be Jack's prize either.

If it was all a lie, I needed to know.

I needed it to be a lie.

All of it.

As if it were even possible, the storm had gotten worse. I forced everything out of my mind and concentrated on the road. The tracks Don and I made this morning were gone. The snow-markers on either side of the road were my only guides. I felt as if I were floating in a sea of cold shadows and deceit, of betrayal and deception.

Through the driving snow, I found the turnoff to the ranch. I'd assumed it was Jack who needed help. What if it was Jane? Or both? This could only get worse.

The main house sat still and dark. I followed the tire tracks around back, past the barn where we'd found the oil and up the slope toward the trees. The snow was deep. Jack's truck was in four-wheel drive, and there was extra weight in the bed, so I was able to make it.

I slowed. Through the falling snow, I could barely make out the tracks leading straight up to the trees.

I passed a half-collapsed barn. Like a dead relic of another era, the bare bones of the structure stuck out of the snow.

Dead.

Under the tall Ponderosas, behind a growth of smaller pines sat an old clapboard structure. Probably the original ranch house. Sheets of plywood covered the front windows. With no light showing the little place was invisible under the dark tree line. When I'd first seen the B&B, two of the front windows had been boarded up, broken out as a warning to my dad to stop or worse would happen. *Worse had* happened. Anxiety filled me; I couldn't survive the death of the man... I sighed and gave in to the truth. The man I loved.

What lay behind the warped, paint-bare front door? The image of the blood-covered notes brought back the memory of my dad bleeding to death in my arms. Of his life slipping away as I held him, helpless to prevent the inevitable. Would this beat up house hold more death? And what kind; physical or emotional?

With the water bottles in hand and Jack's aid bag over my shoulders, I trudged toward the house. It seemed absurd to knock.

As soon as I stepped onto the porch, the door swung open. Mrs. Shaw waved me inside with the barrel of her shotgun. "What's in there?" She pointed her gun at the aid bag.

"You told me someone was injured. These are my supplies."

"You have a gun?" She poked me so hard in the stomach with the barrel of her weapon I dropped a water bottle.

As I bent to pick it up, I saw a man in the far corner. He was shrouded in shadow, but I could see his silhouette leaning against the wall. He wasn't like the others. There was a kind of calm purpose about him. Everyone else had a sort of enthusiastic confusion. They all frightened me.

"Do you have a gun?" She asked again.

"No." Of course I did. I'd buried it in the bottom of the aid bag. I'd concealed it in what I hoped would pass for a container of bandages. The problem would come when I needed it. "Where are they?"

She patted me down. "Open it." She pointed to the aid bag, which is the Army's version of a huge backpack. A heavy one.

"It'll take too long. If they're in as bad a shape as you say, I need to get to them. Besides, I'm not doing anything stupid with a shotgun pointed at me."

Mrs. Shaw glanced over at the man in the shadows.

"Search it," he ordered.

I held my breath as she rummaged through the items.

"Be careful I need those things clean and unopened." I snatched away a container of pain medication.

"Where's my money?" she demanded as she pushed the bag toward me.

I suppressed my relief at her ineptness. "I still don't have proof of life. Like I told you, no proof no money. And if one of them is dead, the people with the cash have instructions not to pay you." I hoped the lie didn't show on my face.

"I'll kill you and the others." She raised the double barrel shotgun to my face.

"Stop," the man in the corner said in a commanding voice.

I didn't turn. Right now, I had to get to Jack and Jane. "Then it's in both our best interests that we all stay alive," I said as I stuffed things back in the backpack.

"One's in here." Mrs. Shaw indicated the hallway. She shoved me toward the first room on the right.

I stumbled. The aid bag was heavier than I remembered. A man in a blue shirt appeared at the door. When he saw me, he stepped aside. Jane lay on the dirty floor, her hands, feet, and mouth bound. Blood ran down her face from her blackened eye. I bent down and gently removed the duct tape. It had hidden her bruised and swollen mouth. "I'm sorry." I brushed her bloody hair from her face. "Are you hurt anywhere else?" I felt along her arms.

"Don't worry about me." Tracks of tears stained her face. "Boss," she whispered. "I think they killed Jack."

I squeezed my eyes shut. Please, God, no. I struggled to push my emotions to the side. The effort became impossible. I pulled a cold pack from the bag and applied it to Jane's face.

She leaned into me and buried her face in my shoulder. I put my arms around her. "He's been screaming ever since I got here." She pulled back. "They've done something horrible. He's been quiet for a while."

"I'm going to get us out of here." I rubbed her back.

"Ouch." She winced.

There was an abrasion across her shoulder. I felt a cold pain in my gut. I didn't ask her what happened, I had to stay focused. I hoped I could. "Are you going to be okay while I check on Jack?"

"I'm all right." She stiffened. "I'm a country girl. I've been hurt worse."

I knew she was putting on a brave face for me. I squeezed her hand. "I know you are." I faced the two by the door. "Get the tape off her and take me to Jack."

Chapter Twelve

The worn floorboards protested as Mrs. Shaw ushered me through the empty living room. The man in the corner was gone. In the battered kitchen, the linoleum was cracked and worn through to the filthy boards beneath. The cupboard doors hung on broken hinges or were missing entirely. She pointed to a narrow paint-bare door in the corner. "He's down there." Jack hadn't rated an area upstairs.

I didn't look at her. What kind of a poisoned mind could do this?

Outside the wind screeched with fury as it battered the old structure. I could feel the frigid air bleed through the cracks around the windows.

The hinges on the battered door groaned as the rank smell of rot escaped from below.

The wooden treads in front of me looked as if they'd been traveled a million times. With each step, the boards gave a hollow groan. My heart beat harder and faster with each footstep. All I could see below was a small area of the dirt floor and the stone wall beyond.

I reached the last step and turned; the reality of Jack's prison spread out in front of me. It was dank, cold and the stone walls were black with decay.

Suspended in the center of the miserable underground room a naked bulb dangled from the ceiling, beneath it, Jack hung by his wrists. His head drooped forward.

I knew where the blood on the notes had come from. He had a cut above his left temple and several open wounds. He had a long bruise across the left side of his ribs. They were at the least badly bruised, probably fractured. I hoped he didn't have internal injuries too. I touched his shoulder and he groaned. I hoped they weren't dislocated.

Mr. Shaw stepped from the shadows. "Not so pretty anymore, is he?"

I stood in the dirt in front of Jack. My hand shook as I reached up to check for a pulse. His skin felt alarmingly cold, but he was alive.

Dried blood clung to cuts on his forehead, lip, and ear. His shins were terribly beaten and bloody. What caused my heart to seize was the car battery on the floor at his feet. What had they put him through? Then I saw the burns on the inside of his thighs. My heart stopped. No wonder Jane had heard him cry out. This wasn't retaliation for someone's arrest. This was sadistic. I moved behind him. They'd beaten his back raw.

I moved in front of him and put my hand to his battered face. "Jack, can you hear me?"

He moaned as I touched his face.

I turned to the others. "Get him upstairs. If he doesn't die of his injuries, he will from hypothermia." I faced Mrs. Shaw. "Then, it isn't going to be jail it'll be the death penalty. And if they don't give it to you, they'll give it to me for your deaths."

"They'll have to catch me first."

With more hate than I knew I had in me I said, "You're underestimating me. I can not only kill you I can do it in ways that will cause you unimaginable pain." I stopped. Had I gone too far?

"Well, I'm not dying for you." Blue-shirt, the man who'd stood by Jane's door upstairs said as he stepped around me. "Jimmy, grab this guy's other arm."

Jimmy, the hotel clerk, moved out from behind Mr. Shaw.

"You lied to me. You little—" I stopped. The situation was bad enough. I didn't need to be stupid and make things worse.

"Yeah, well. *I'm* not afraid of you. That CIA guy and his big gun aren't here."

Idiot. He was dealing with a desperate angry woman. I was so much more dangerous than some *CIA guy* with a *big gun*.

Blue-shirt cut the ropes holding Jack's wrists. He fell to the filthy floor. I went to him.

"Get out of the way if you want us to get him upstairs," Blue-shirt said. He and Jimmy struggled as they dragged Jack up the steps.

»§«

They dropped him on the floor next to Jane.

"Before you fix him up, I want my money," Mrs. Shaw demanded.

"Your biggest problem right now is whether I can save him." I had to stall her. Once they found there wasn't any money, I wasn't sure what would happen.

"No. I want the cash now. All I had to do was show you they were both alive," Mrs. Shaw's voice teetered on the edge of hysteria. I could understand anger or anxiety, but why the near frenzy?

"My people have instructions not to deliver the money if either of them is dead."

"Fine, make sure he doesn't die," Mrs. Shaw pointed at Jack.

"Something you might have considered before your friends nearly beat him to death." Behind me, I heard Jane sniff back tears. "Get me some blankets. I've got to raise his body temperature."

She shouted at Jimmy to get a blanket. To me, "Fix him." She slammed the door behind her.

"Is he dead?" Jane brushed tears from her eyes.

"No. I'm going to do everything I can to keep him alive." I took off my jacket and covered him as much as I could. Then, I pulled out the space blanket and spread it over the rest of him. His pulse was weak, his breathing was shallow, and he was still unconscious. Hypothermia became my primary concern.

Mrs. Shaw came back and threw a dirty blanket at us. This time, when she left, she slammed the door so hard it popped back open.

I covered Jack. I was glad the space blanket was between him and the filthy one. "What's with these animals?"

"I don't know." Jane brushed her tears away. "You didn't want an answer, did you?"

"Talk to me, tell me what happened." I needed the sound of her voice. A voice that was always reassuring.

"Mrs. Shaw is mean. But the one who scares me the most is her skinny husband. I know he's the one who did all this to Jack. She was up here when I heard—" Jane cradled Jack's hand in hers.

"Why did they take you?" There was no apparent reason for targeting her.

"They said they wanted to get you to pay them." She glanced down at Jack. "That doesn't make sense, they already had Jack."

"This is more complicated than we know. As far as I can tell only a few people understand what's really going on and none of them will tell me." There was little I could do in this grimy area. I could clean his wounds, but he needed an emergency room. One equipped with all the things I didn't have.

"You can save him, can't you? You've got to."

"From what I can see his injuries are bad but not life threatening." I didn't want to worry her with the *what if's* of internal damage. "I'm most worried about the hypothermia." I handed her one of the bottles of water. "Drink some of this." I took the second bottle and some cotton from the aid bag. I pulled Jack's phone from the bottom compartment and slipped it in my pocket. Done, I moistened the cotton. "Clean the blood from his face as best you can. I need to see to the cut on his head." It would give her something to concentrate on besides the three of us dying. Besides the cold, I was worried about the bruise on his chest. I needed him conscious. "Jack, wake up." I put my hand on his cheek. "Come on." I smoothed my hand along the side of his face that wasn't bloody.

He moaned and moved his head toward me, but he didn't come around. I searched through the aid bag for an ammonia inhalant. After I snapped it, I waved it under his nose. "Jack, wake up."

He opened his eyes. "Doc."

"How badly are you hurt?"

"Cracked ribs. I hurt everywhere." He tensed as he raised his hand to his injured chest.

His words were slurred. Not good. "Relax and tell me what they used on you?" It wasn't morbid curiosity. I needed to know. If it was metal, the damage would be worse than if it was a hose.

"A wooden dowel on my chest and shins. I don't know what they beat me with." He tried to sit up. "Where am I?" Then he saw Jane. "What the hell's going on?"

"Lay down. I need you to be still." Wood would hurt, but it wouldn't do the damage a metal pipe would.

He took my hand. "Doc, you and Jane need to get out of here."

"Leave you behind? Hell, no." Mad had stolen Jane's tears. "I couldn't live with myself. Besides, what would I tell Stan and Lois?" She shook her head. "No."

"Jack, you know I'm not leaving you here. I didn't abandon you when we were up on the mountain, and I won't now."

"I can't let *him* get to you. With my shins battered I won't get ten yards."

"Will you lay still?" This was far, far worse than when we'd been stuck in the hills in October. We'd had hope, then. He could walk. Now, I had no idea how I was going to get him out of here. "Can't let who get to me?" I was afraid he was getting delirious from the cold.

"Did you call Brad?" he asked.

"Yes. Now, please let me look at your injuries." I wasn't going to tell him the FBI wouldn't be coming to the rescue this time.

No one would.

I was it.

I was everyone's last best hope.

He shivered. "No. I have to say this. I'm not going to—"

"Not going to what? Make it? Really? The big war hero who swoops in and rescues a group of little girls against all odds is going to give up?" I drew in a breath. "Well? Are you?"

He sank back to the floor. "What did March tell you?"

"It isn't important. I have to know how badly you're hurt." He'd know. "Do you think your wrists are broken?" I took a stabilizing breath. It didn't work I still trembled inside.

"I don't know." He shivered again. "God, I'm cold."

He flinched when I touched his shoulder. That was probably from being strung up all night and day. "Let me see your wrists."

He took them out from under my jacket. They were swollen from the stress of hanging. The rope had chafed the skin leaving it raw and bleeding. "I can't tell if they're broken." I found some lidocaine ointment and spread it on the abrasions. It would take away some of the pain, but it wouldn't last long.

I pulled my jacket and the blanket back around his shoulders. Then moved the blanket from his legs. I saw the burns from the battery on the inside of his thighs. I hardened my heart as I spread the lidocaine on them. There wasn't much I could do for his shins. His legs weren't broken, but they had to be unbearably painful. They were bruised from his feet to his knees. In a couple of places, the skin was broken.

I clenched my jaw. These people were going to pay.

Every damn one of them.

Jane had finished cleaning his face. "Can we carry him?"

We both turned to her.

"No," Jack said.

She shook her head. "Probably not."

Jack closed his eyes.

Keep him talking, I mouthed to Jane, as I parted his hair. The cut needed stitches. I put a butterfly on it to stop the bleeding.

"Jack Trace, I have a fresh turkey ready for the oven. How are you going to sit at the Christmas dinner table with all those bumps and cuts?"

"Aunt Jane. I wouldn't be able to eat, I'm too cold."

His speech was more slurred. He was succumbing to the hypothermia.

I angled Jack's head toward me. I stared into his crystalline hazel eyes. The one's I'd gazed into as he'd lied to me, and I'd believed him. Or had he? "Jack," I whispered. My goal right now was to get him out of here and to the hospital. I'd deal with Don's story later. I pulled two hand warmers out of the pack and placed them over his Femoral arteries. It would help warm him.

"We need a plan." Jane glanced at the door. "What if we move the dresser in front of the door?" She shook her head. "The bullets will go right through the walls."

"Let us help you sit up; I need to wrap your ribs. It'll help with the pain so we can get you out of here."

The three of us struggled to get him up. He laid his head on my shoulder like he had time and again in the past two months. Then it had sent a wave of warmth and comfort through me. Now I didn't know what to feel. Was this the Jack I needed him to be? Or was he the killer and womanizer Don said he was?

It took a couple of minutes, but I got his ribs wrapped. "I know this is going to hurt the bruises and scrapes on your back, but it will keep your ribs stable." I put my jacket around his shoulders. He didn't let go of me.

Instead, he gently held me. I could feel his lips on my neck as he spoke, "Ens."

"Lay back."

"No. I need to say this."

"You don't need to say anything." The sharpness in my voice surprised me as much as it did him.

The door burst open, and Mrs. Shaw stormed in. "We searched the truck. Money's not coming, is it? Or is it in that?" She pointed to the aid bag.

Chapter Thirteen

I couldn't let her take the bag. Hidden in it was Jack's 40 cal. "You didn't think I was going to bring it with me, did you? Besides, everything is closed. It's Christmas." Or haven't you heard?

"There's no money, is there?" She pointed her shotgun at Jack. "He's first."

I stood and moved between her and Jack.

Having a gun aimed at you point blank, is scary as hell. I mean your-life-flashes-in-front-of-your-eyes petrifying. A shotgun is a hundred times worse. No, a thousand times when a crazy person is on the trigger end. "If you kill us there's no chance, you'll get anything, but a long prison sentence. The town is snowed in, you can't get out before they find you." I figured she was at least smart enough to understand that.

"Have your big-time CIA friend call the government and get it," Jimmy shouted from behind Mrs. Shaw.

"Yeah, call him. I want my money." She pushed me with the barrel of the gun.

I stood my ground between Mrs. Shaw and Jack. "It's Christmas everywhere, they're not open, either." Didn't she watch the news? The government didn't negotiate with terrorists. And this group was about as terrifying as it got. Maybe if I pointed out the obvious. "The only way I can get the money is to sell everything I have. It'll take weeks. Months."

"Then, I want the diamonds. I know he has diamonds." She motioned toward Jack.

That caught me off guard. Wait, how did she know about them? Was she guessing? No, I don't believe in coincidence. Her demand brought a whole new dimension to everything. The only mention of diamonds had been in Don's version of the mission in Africa. No one here could possibly know about that mission. Could they? Don. I clenched my fists. Damn him, he'd held back information. "Diamonds?"

"I know he has a stash of diamonds and cash. I want it all."

She wasn't guessing, her demand was too close to Don's story. Besides, I'd never heard any rumors of either diamonds or cash. "Diamonds?" I asked again. And yes, I was playing dumb.

She nodded toward the hall. "He told me all about the money and the gems."

He?

At that moment, someone grabbed Jimmy from the doorway. A few seconds later he stumbled back into the room. His eyes were wide with fear. "You weren't supposed to tell her about that."

I heard the front door slam shut.

"I don't care what he wants." She hadn't taken her eyes off me. "I want my money." Her finger moved to the trigger.

My thoughts jostled into place and a plan of sorts formed. "Okay, you win." I had to keep her from pulling the trigger. "The safe at Jack's house has a palm imprint release mechanism." With us out of here, I could get Jack warm, and I'd buy some time to figure out what to do next.

"Fine. We'll cut off his hand."

I gasped as I heard Jane give a little cry. My brain raced to come up with something plausible. "That won't work." Yes, I was banking on the fact she didn't know any more about palm imprint safes than I did. I wasn't a hundred percent sure such a thing existed outside of the movie industry. I knew it was possible to open your phone with a thumbprint. I'd seen the commercials. So, what the hell? "It reads body temperature and galvanic skin response as well as the print. If those three things aren't present, the safe won't open. If you try to break into it, a device will destroy everything inside. Money and all." My bluff had to work.

"So, no cutting off anything," Jane said.

"Here's what's going to happen." Since she bought my 'I'm lying' expression for confidence I figured I might as well go for broke. "The FBI and Homeland are working their way here. So, if you're quick and smart,"—fat chance on either count—"you'll have a head start."

"No one's getting through this storm—Mrs. Shaw bellowed. "I want that money."

"I got a call right after yours. An FBI agent, by the name of Brad Hughes, just landed in Jackson Hole. You remember him. He's the one who arrested your father." I was trying to rattle her enough to keep her off balance so she couldn't think straight. I had to be careful not to push too many of her buttons. After all, she still had a shotgun aimed at my gut. "From the other side, the CIA is working its way up from Boise." I prayed my poker face—which I know I don't have—held.

Someone in the hall called to her, and she left the room.

I let out the breath I'd been holding and went to Jack and Jane. "There are clean blankets in the back of the truck. We'll try to get you warm." I touched his cheek. "You're going to be fine. Your 40 cal. is in the bottom of the aid bag. I can't get to it without getting us all killed. Maybe one of you'll have a chance in the truck."

Mrs. Shaw entered the room. "Okay, we take two trucks," her voice was high with excitement. "Granny goes with you and me. Moneybags goes with Nate, TJ, and Jimmy." That left out Shadow-man. Had he been the slamming door a few minutes ago?

Splitting us up was out of the question. And I wasn't going to let her scummy husband, Nate, near Jack again. "No. Jack goes with us. Jane's a nurse." I figured in for a penny… "He needs an I.V. She has to keep it warm and hold it. If it isn't held right, he'll get air in his vein and die and then you won't get your diamonds or money."

She glanced out the door, then nodded. "Fine. I ride with you."

Good, Mr. Sadist wouldn't be with us.

"Where are Jack's clothes?" I asked.

"He never had a shirt. His pants are in the basement somewhere." She called over her shoulder, "TJ, get this guy's pants. Now."

TJ aka Blue-shirt came in and tossed Jack's pants to me.

I helped Jack sit up. We got his pants on over his battered legs. The pain washed-out the remaining color in his face until his skin was ghost-white, he had to hurt like hell. "I'm sorry," I whispered. "Let me give you a shot for the pain."

He squeezed my hand. "No."

I pulled a liter of saline out of the aid bag.

"This is new since October," I said.

"I figured I needed to prepare a little more after our picnic." Jack's words were still slurred, and he was shaking so hard we could barely get him dressed. As we carefully slipped his pants on

I flashed back to the two of us stranded in the mountains as we shared the lunch Jane had packed. He'd promised to take me on a proper picnic in the summer. Don's story raced through my mind. I didn't know what to say. I didn't want to think about Africa. About Jack's deception. If indeed, there was one. Oh, God, this was so hard. My heart held all the frenzy of the raging blizzard outside.

This was up to Jane and me. I taped the tubing to his arm, then covered it with gauze, and secured it with more tape. I hoped my attempt at faking the I.V. worked. If he had to protect himself—if he could—I didn't want anything ripping into his vein.

Jane and I got Jack to his feet. I wrapped the space blanket around his body. He put his arm around me. I remembered the soft autumn day up in the hills. Our struggle to survive. The memory of our first kiss in the hospital when we were safe. All his kisses since then. Every memory—all of it—marred by Don's story.

No. I owed it to Jack to hear his side. He once told me there's an element of truth in every lie. I struggled to harden my heart. It didn't work. I felt it breaking.

Jane and I got him in the back of the truck and secured the blankets around him.

Mrs. Shaw sat in the passenger's seat sideways. Her shotgun pointed at Jack. Getting to the 40 cal. was out.

»§«

Jack's house appeared dark and lonely. I remembered the night I'd come here to confront him about his involvement in the resort scandal. The house had been lit with the warmth of friendship. He'd met me at the front door with a simple, "Hi." My heart melted at the memory of the smile on his face, and the tenderness in his eyes. As if I were the only person in the world he cared about. The image of him and Lois standing in the doorway always made me smile. Not the big broad smile of humor, but the soft, gentle smile that comes with being in love. Yes, I've given up any pretense I was anything but in love. How was I going to survive this if it was all a lie? "No." The word slipped out in a breath.

"What?" Mrs. Shaw demanded.

Focus. "Nothing."

»§«

I pulled to a stop at Jack's and shut off the engine. The wreath we'd selected last week hung on the front door. Those seven days now seemed like a lifetime ago.

If I was going to die, I wanted to know my killer's name. "What's your name? I mean your real name." Brad hadn't said which of the three names he'd given me was real. I figured the ones on the registration card at the B&B were fake.

"What? Why do you care?"

"Because referring to you as Mrs. Shaw in my head is getting tiresome."

She blinked at me. "Alice. Alice Shaw."

"Fine, Alice. Let's get this over with." There was a lot more bravado in my words than in my heart. Hey, if I'm going out, I'm going with dignity. I'm not crawling for anyone.

My SUV sat where Don and I left it earlier. The snow covered it.

I helped Jack out of the backseat. He put his arms around me. "Ens, you have to listen to me."

"Later." The word came out dismissively.

"No, now." He held onto me. "In the library, there's a picture above a set of glass bookcase doors. Open it, there's a gun in the recess. Kill as many of them as you can. I'll do my best."

"You can't do anything, if you have a broken rib, you could puncture a lung. I can't get you to the hospital fast enough in this weather. You'll die."

"But you'll be safe."

"I'm not going to let you die." I needed to hear the truth from him. I knew he wouldn't lie to me. But if he'd done everything Don said he had, why wouldn't he? I felt my heart quicken. I couldn't be wrong again.

Not this time.

"Ens, I'm not worth it. I know what Don was going to tell you. It's the truth. You should be with a good man. Someone who'll love you and take care of you. Not me. It's what I was going to tell you last night. I was breaking it off."

My heart shattered.

Irretrievably crushed.

The pain ripped at my soul and stole my courage.

An involuntary sob escaped me. "Fine." What was I going to say? "At least you were honest with me." I struggled to keep my voice even. "I'll go back to D.C., and my old life. Idaho hasn't been all that great to me." This wound was deep. I reminded myself I'd only known him a couple of months. Ten weeks. I swallowed the crushing pain I wasn't sure I could endure.

Inside, Jack said, "It's in the library."

TJ and Jimmy were on either side of Jack. Between the hypothermia and his injuries, it took a few minutes to get to the hall and into the cozy room.

Alice spun on her skinny husband. "If you hadn't beat the crap out of him, this would have been a lot easier." She smacked him hard on the back of the head.

Probably what was wrong with him, too many blows to the head.

I reached for the picture over the bookcase.

"Stop." Alice seized my wrist with the same cruel hand she'd struck her husband with. "I don't trust you." She pushed me to the side and clutched at the picture frame.

I glanced over at Jack. He shook his head. I didn't know if it meant all was lost, or we were switching to plan 'B.' He always had one. He just hadn't shared it with me. It seemed there were a lot of things he hadn't shared. I swallowed my tears.

"What's this?" Alice snatched the gun from behind the picture. With one swift motion, she slapped me hard enough to knock me into the table between the leather wingback chairs.

The pain of the slap and the toxic events of the day had unwanted tears welling up in my eyes.

"Ah, is the big tough doctor going to cry for us? Now, isn't this precious? Poor little rich girl. Are we supposed to feel sorry for you?" She snatched my hair and wrenched my head back as she jammed the barrel of the gun into my throat.

"No." It was her husband Mr. Tall-skinny-and-disgusting. "I want her."

The prospect sent a lightning bolt of terror through me. I'd seen what he'd done to Jack. I cringed as the image of the car battery sitting on the floor inches from Jack slipped through my consciousness.

Chapter Fourteen

"You want what?" Alice screamed, her face red with rage, her free hand clinched, and her gun hand slowly raising.

Mr. Disgusting took a step toward me. "Her. I've never had a pretty woman before." Nate licked his greedy lips.

I pulled free from Alice's grasp. It didn't take much since her attention was focused on her stupid spouse.

"What do you mean? You've never had a pretty woman?" Alice stared at her miserable excuse for a husband.

He'd taken one crazy step too far. He'd just told his wife she wasn't pretty. No woman wants to hear those words from her husband. Ever.

He grabbed me by the arm and jerked me to him. His foul breath washed over my face as his grip tightened on my arm. He had the kind of strength insanity provides. He tried to kiss me as he groped my breasts.

I searched around with my free hand for something, anything, to hit him with. As it turned out, I didn't need to.

"No." Alice pulled me back. Between us both pulling, he let go.

Out of the corner of my eye, I caught a movement behind Mr. Crazy. Jack had managed to get to his feet. Mr. Crazy was still off balance from our tug-of-war. In the same split second, Jack snapped the man's neck, and Alice fired. She hit her skinny husband in the chest as Jack let him fall to the floor.

Alice stood open-mouthed as she held up the gun and realized what she'd done. I took the revolver from her before she came to her senses.

The blow I delivered came with all the pent-up anger, hurt, and torment I'd experienced in the past twenty-four hours. Alice went down like a bag of doorknobs. I was pretty sure the gun in my hand helped in the process.

"Leave before—" Jack struggled to stay on his feet.

"I'm not going anywhere," Jane announced as she removed the gun Mr. Scary had tucked under his belt.

Jack leaned hard on the wingback chair. "Doc, I want you and Jane to get the hell out of here. Now," the word came out in a gasp as he held his ribs.

We both stared at him.

"No." I didn't wait for his protest. "Jane, shoot her if she gets up." I left the library and walked down the hall. "Nice move," I said out loud. "Now what?"

I decided to take my anger out on the first person I came across. I had no idea where the other two were. Or, what I'd do when I found them. Then I heard a truck start outside.

Through the dining room windows, I saw Jack's truck fishtail down the driveway. Great, truck number two gone. That was going to make him mad. A mad I wouldn't be here to see.

I glanced out the front door. The truck Nate, Jimmy, and TJ had followed us in still sat out front. With Jimmy trying to start it. "Out." I leveled my gun at him. "Now."

He ground on the starter.

"Don't push me. I will shoot your ass."

He turned terrified eyes my way. I guess he finally figured out who was more dangerous, the big CIA guy or the desperate woman. He made another effort to start the truck.

It wouldn't catch.

Completely out of patience

I walked over, jerked open the door and grabbed him out of the truck. Adrenalin is a great asset when you're not big. He landed in the snow.

"Get up." I pulled Jack's cell phone out of my pocket. It felt so heavy; I didn't know if I could hold it one second more. I'd gripped it tight all night, hoping Don was wrong. With Jack's confession, the crushing pain in my heart became unbearable. I gasped. My hand shook as I dialed the Sheriff's Office. "Phyllis, get an ambulance out to Jack's as fast as you can. Tell Don to get out here, too."

"Did you find Jack? Is he alive?"

"I did and, yes, he's still alive. But he's in bad shape."

I marched Jimmy back in the house.

Jack, Jane, and Alice were still in the library.

Jane held Alice at gunpoint. "Here's one more for you." I shoved Jimmy at Alice. He landed hard against the bookshelf.

Jack now lied on the floor. He'd used his last ounce of strength to kill Mr. Creepy. I knew how much power it took to break a man's neck. Jack's technique had been smooth and powerful. The effort had left him in physical distress. Now his eyes were glassy, and his breathing labored. "Lie still. An ambulance is on the way." I wanted to touch him. I couldn't. The feeling of betrayal overwhelmed me.

Defeat dulled his eyes. "Thanks," was all he said as he looked away.

Good. I wasn't in the mood for conversation either. What would I say? He'd done exactly what Don told me he would. Sort of. He'd let me go. Why? I mean... it didn't make sense. Something niggled at my exhausted brain. But he'd said Don's version was right, and he was letting me go.

The faux fur throw I'd teased him about just yesterday still lay on the wing backed chair. I laid it over him. "You'll be fine."

"Ens—"

"Don't. Don't you ever call me that again. Do you hear me? Ever. You've said enough. Done enough. I get it. Your wish is granted, I'm leaving." I put his phone on the floor beside him.

He lie there. On his beautiful hardwood floor in his beautiful home. Where he lived all alone.

I walked away, through the area between the living and dining rooms, and out the front door. I stopped at the sight of the wreath. I hated it. I hated what had happened tonight. I hated myself for being so naive. And I hated Jack for not being who I thought he was. I grabbed the wreath from the door and threw it with all the anguish slashing at my broken heart.

Don drove up in one of the Sheriff's SUV's. He left the door open as he jumped out and ran to me. He reached out for me. "Ensley, are—"

I hurried past him. I blamed him for everything. I knew he had a hand in all this misery. He'd sent Jack on missions he was sure Jack couldn't survive. But why? What had happened between them to foster the hate they had for each other? It didn't matter now; I was closing this chapter of my life.

I mentioned before how I hate to cry. Well, I hate to cry uncontrollably even more.

»§«

Through my tears, I missed the keyhole in my front door twice before I got it unlocked. In my bedroom, the cats were asleep on my bed. "Mason." I sat next to him. He stretched and rubbed his face against my arm. "I'm leaving."

I pushed Sophie's icon on my phone. I told her everything.

"E's come home. Mama and I are here for you."

I packed and unpacked and packed again. All I could hear was Jack telling me he didn't want me anymore. His words played over and over in my head. I kept telling myself I'd be okay in time. I even said the words out loud.

The problem was the hurt. It wasn't only heartbreak, this was deeper. Much deeper. I felt as if the essence of my soul had been ripped from me.

Jane walked in and without a word, she wrapped her arms around me.

I hugged her back and asked. "Has loved lied to me again?"

Epilogue

I snapped my towel at the counter. This Christmas had turned out all wrong. Real wrong. The Boss was gone, and Jack was hurt, and Stan... well, he wasn't here. I stared at the turkey no one was going to be here to eat. I snapped my towel at the counter.

At least Mrs. Shaw, Jimmy, and TJ were in jail. The problem was the other man. The one who stayed in the shadows. He'd disappeared. How could he when the whole area had been snowed in until this morning?

"No point in wasting the bird," I told the cats. I turned on the oven as I heard the back-door open. I glanced up. "Jack Trace." I put my hands on my hips. "You're supposed to be in the hospital. I heard the doctor tell you two days. That was last night. And by the way, you look terrible. Did you even sleep?" My kitchen seems to be the place everyone ends up. Good thing it's a big one.

"Thanks, Aunt Jane. I don't like hospitals. I hurt, but it was mostly the hypothermia. I needed to warm up for a while. I have a few cracked ribs, and my shins are killing me, but I've been in worse shape." He leaned against the old worn counter. "I could use some of your orange tea." He smiled, but it didn't reach his eyes.

I took two mugs and my special plate down from the shelf. "You going to tell me what yesterday was all about?" I poured a cup of tea for each of us and brought out a few cookies. Not the ones the Boss and I had made . Neither of us needed to be reminded it was Christmas Day. Besides, half of them had been crushed by those people when they came for me. What was left still sat in the container under the tall windows. I'd covered them with a towel. "We can't have tea without cookies." I got out the molasses treats and set them on the plate between us.

"Thanks." There was no life in his voice, and the light had gone out in his eyes. I knew it wasn't from the physical pain. This hurt came from deep down inside.

There'd be no Christmas for any of us this year. The Boss had come home last night and cried till dawn. This morning, when we were supposed to be at Jack's enjoying each other's company, she was headed for Boise right behind the snowplow. I glanced over at the window. I'd take the cookies down to the old folk's home. I didn't want them sitting around here reminding me of the worst Christmas ever.

"I don't want you standing there." I moved a stool over by the window for him. "I saw your legs. Sit." When two scared people are in love someone has to give them a shove. I figured the pushing was up to me since Stan wasn't here. "Now. What are you going to do about it?"

"About what?"

"Jack Trace, you know as well as I do about what."

He didn't look up from his tea. "Where is she?" He sounded like a man who'd had his heart and soul torn from him.

"Gone. She packed a bag and drove to Boise. She's flying back to D.C., this afternoon." I snapped my towel at a crumb on the counter. "I'm supposed to take care of things. She'll send money if I need it. I'm to get paid extra for running the place." I took a breath. "I don't mind telling you I'm not happy about any of this."

"It's better this way."

"Oh? Is that so? For who exactly?"

"For once, he's right." The voice came from behind us.

We both turned. Don March stood in the doorway of my kitchen. I don't like him. I told him so. He said he didn't care.

Jack struggled to his feet. "What did you tell her, March?"

Mr. CIA gave a real nasty smile. "My version of what happened. Africa came back on *you* this time." He folded his arms like he owned the world. "You were right. She didn't believe me." His self-satisfied expression held an extra air of pleasure. "What convinced her I was right?"

"I did," Jack said.

I'd never seen Jack like this. When he'd first gotten here, he was a troubled man, but he'd fought hard and overcame those demons. This was far worse. He'd given up. I could see it in his eyes, hear it in his voice, it was even in the way he stood.

"Trace, I thought you were smarter than that. Guess all—" he stopped and glanced over at me.

"Why was the Phantom here," Jack rubbed his shoulder.

"It must be payback time." Mr. CIA gave a snarl of a smile. "It must be payback time."

"He's had years to get back at me. Why now?"

"I think we both know the answer to that," Mr. CIA said. I wouldn't even say his name in my head. "I got her job back for her at JPL Corp. She'll be safe back there with me."

"I know," what little life had been in Jack washed-out.

I didn't like this surprise at all. "She didn't say anything to me about it." Her leaving had put a big hole in my world. I knew it had torn the very life out of her. I'd never seen a woman in so much pain. Now, I could see what it had cost Jack, too. It was evident to anyone looking, he was in loved.

"I know it's what's best for her. I know her better than you do, Trace. I *know* her a lot better."

I understood exactly what he meant by *know*. The Boss shouldn't be with this ass.

"She was going to marry me." He looked Jack right in the eye. "She will now. I'll tell her hello for you when I see her."

Jack shook his head. "You think she'll be waiting for you. She won't. You have no idea who she really is."

"You're wrong again, I'll win her back. My lifestyle is what she's used to. Not this dust trap you live in."

This man was mean—cruel to his core. How could the Boss ever think he was worth caring for?

"Go ahead, March. Gloat." Jack leveled a glare right back at him. "You finally beat me. Too bad you couldn't do it honorably, but then you've never let integrity stand in your way. She left me, but make no mistake, she isn't running to you. We both lost. Zero to zero."

"We'll see. I'm leaving as soon as I settle my bill." Mr. CIA pulled out his wallet. "You can have this worthless town all to yourself."

Jack stood a little taller. "March." A smile bent his lips. "You get your new condo for her? The one you closed on the day before you got here?" He took a step forward. "I hope you like it at 4327 West Elm Avenue. Too bad it was a waste of money. She'll never live there."

A flash of fear passed over Mr. CIA's face. It was instantly replaced with anger. Then, he gave a smug smile. "I know the truth. Too bad she never will."

This guy was no match for Jack. He may have a fancy CIA job in Washington, but I knew if it came down to it, Jack would always win. He had to win this time, too. He couldn't let the Boss go this easy. I hoped they'd realize they loved each other before it was too late. I didn't want them to lose what I had once.

This pompous ass had stayed long enough. I pushed Mr. CIA out into the dining room and handed him his bill. "If she chooses you— which she won't—and you hurt her, and if Jack doesn't come for you, I will. I was Idaho Women's Sharpshooting Champ five years in a row. I don't miss ever."

"You people are all crazy." He shoved a wad of cash at me and left without another word.

The front door slammed behind him. "Good. One problem down." Now I had to get the important matter straightened out.

In the kitchen, I found Jack staring out the window at Mr. CIA getting into his car.

I'm a curious sort, so I asked. "What was that about a new condo?"

"Just my way of letting him know I have connections. He got the point."

These guys had their own way of getting things across. Wait... *still have connections?* He wasn't in the Army, anymore was he? I looked up at him. He is a man with secrets.

"I want her to be happy," Jack said as he watched the car drive away.

I noticed he hadn't said her name once. From the sadness on his face, I figured he couldn't. "I don't think I've ever seen a man so miserable."

"Aunt Jane." He gazed down at me. "What have I done?"

"As far as I can tell, you've been a damned fool, Jack Trace. You need to go put this straight. It's real inconvenient for me when she's gone." I missed her already. "And what about the cats? They aren't happy without her."

"You don't understand. I told her Don's story was the truth, and I didn't want her."

"You did what?" My voice was too loud. I shook my head. How could two such smart people be so damn dumb? All he had to do was go after her and tell her the truth. "Why in God's good name would you do such a stupid thing?"

He sat down. "It's complicated."

"Everything is with you two."

"This is my past coming back on me. I may deserve it, but she doesn't."

I needed him to flesh that out a bit. "You know Stan tells me everything." Okay, that wasn't strictly true, but I supposed he would if I asked.

"I need her to be safe," was all he said.

"Even if it breaks her heart... and yours?"

"All I've done, since she's been here, is put her life in danger." He wrapped his hands around his cup. "When she stepped between that crazy woman with a shotgun and me..." He picked up a cookie then laid it back down. "It's all I can think about. When I close my eyes, it's all I can see. She put her life on the line for me." He picked up the cookie again and laid it on the counter by his mug. "What if the woman had flinched and pulled the trigger? She'd be dead, and I'd have no hope. Aunt Jane, I've never felt this way about anyone. I can't

—I'd rather live the rest of my life alone than put her in danger again. I want... no, I need her to be safe and happy."

I could tell he had more to say. "What's the rest of it?"

"You are an amazing woman." Jack shook his head. "There was another man there. He was calling the shots. He knew how to inflict the most pain with the least amount of damage. "I hope I'm wrong, or it was the pain, but I recognized him, even with a hood over my head most of the time."

"How can you know that if you couldn't see him?" I asked.

"It was his technique and the fact that he didn't ask me any questions. It could only be one man, and he's dangerous. If I'm right, he knows about her now." He covered my hand with his. "If she'd stayed, he'd go after her. If she isn't with me, she'll have no value to him. No matter what it cost me, I couldn't let him get to her. That's why I had to make her leave me."

I was going to call him on this. He had to realize two things; neither of them would ever be happy without the other, and together they were strong enough to handle anything thrown their way. "You'll find another woman." I studied his face.

"No." His voice was so soft I had to strain to hear him. "I've never told anyone this. It doesn't matter, now. After the incident in Africa, I went to Ralph's office. He was packing to return to the States. When I walked in, he was holding a picture of the most beautiful woman I'd ever seen. Despite being forced to give up his command and retire, he was smiling. He said, 'Want to see a picture of my daughter the doctor? I can't believe how she's changed. I guess D.C., agrees with her.' Then he said, 'I never would have guessed she'd like the political life.'"

Jack let my hand go and picked up his cookie, then set it back down. "It wasn't her beauty that held my attention it was her gray eyes so full of warmth. Her genuine smile. It had a shy quality, as if she was in an unfamiliar world. She was the embodiment of everything good and wholesome. Long walks in the country, coffee on Saturday morning... God, I needed all the normal I could get. Ralph told me how hard she'd worked to get where she was and about her stubborn streak." He smiled. "She is the most stubborn woman I've ever known.

Do you think it's possible to fall in love with a story and a photo?" He didn't wait for my answer. "I didn't until—" He pulled out his wallet and removed a picture in a worn photo sleeve. "Ralph gave me this that day. I don't know why. A proud dad, I guess." He handed me the picture. "Ever wonder why I was never around when she was here?"

"I did. I thought it was odd; you being so close to Ralph and Stan."

"It wasn't an accident." He rubbed his chest where his ribs hurt. "She deserved more than I could give her then. More than I can give her now. Look what she went through yesterday." He didn't say anything for a time. "When I first got here, I was suffering from PTSD. Those girls, my men... I was dealing with nightmares and depression. I couldn't be with anyone. Hell, *I* was having a hard time being with me. The only things keeping me going were this photo, my job, and Lois. The night Ralph was murdered, I didn't recognize her right away. She was covered with her dad's blood. When I did." He sipped his tea and moved his cookie around. I waited for him to go on. "I was afraid she'd be nothing more than a beautiful face in a picture. A fantasy. One I'd conjured up to stay sane. I was wrong. She is more than I—." He glanced out the window at the winter cold. "I made a promise to myself a long time ago," he paused. "I'd only get married once. It won't happen now. I could never be with anyone else."

I saw something I never thought I would. Tears pooled in his eyes. "Aunt Jane, I don't know how to go on without her."

I needed to put this right. "There's an old woman who knows exactly what Don March told her."

His smile was weak as he asked, "Who is she?"

"Don't you get cute with me, Jack Trace." I let it go. I told him word for word what the Boss had said to me. "Some of it was real hard to make out, she was crying so hard."

He flinched as he took a deep breath. "Damn, March. That story is a lie."

"Are you going to tell me what happened over there?" I watched him over the rim of my cup.

He nodded. "The girl they sent us to rescue had been—" again he fixed his eyes on the snow outside. "The poor kid had been raped so many times, she—" He dropped his head. "She ended up with God knows what and died six months later. Her parents couldn't deal with her death. Her mother crawled into a bottle, and her father ate his gun. A whole family destroyed." He paused. "Most of the rest of the girls are recovering. Some are doing better than others."

"And the one he said you murdered?"

"I told myself it was part of the job. I might have found another way, made a better choice. She left me no option. She'd already put a bullet in me, and she'd aimed her weapon at one of the girls."

"What about all the money and such?"

He studied his tea then said, "Some terrorist in Africa is living it up. When reinforcements arrived, I wasn't going to risk one more life for a bag of rocks. The girls and my team were more important. You can replace cash. Those young people deserved a chance. Five of my men had given their lives so they would survive." He looked from his cup to me. "If it hadn't been for Ralph and Stan doing the right thing, the honorable thing, there'd be forty American bodies rotting in Africa right now."

"How do we put this right?" I knew one thing for sure, he wasn't the kind of man who'd give up no matter how bad the odds were. He had to realize he sat at a crossroads with only one real choice.

He gave me the saddest smile I've ever seen. "I'm not sure we can."

I turned away from the pain on his face and busied myself with more tea. "Jack Trace, you listen to me. She'll be back. She left all her clothes and fancy shoes behind. The cats too. I know the girl's heart after last night. She needs time, but she'll figure out the most important part of her life is sitting right next to me."

He started to say something, but I didn't let him.

"You know it as well as I do." I sighed. These two... "No matter what, she'll be back to hear your side of the story. She is her father's daughter."

"She already thinks she knows. I told her Don's version was the truth."

I gave out a loud sigh this time. "Jack." These two needed a road map. "You know as well as I do how smart she is. She'll turn what Mr. CIA told her over and over in her head. She'll talk to her friend

Sophie, and she'll figure out he lied to her. She already knows what kind of man he is." I pointed my finger at him. "She knows what kind of man you are too. Now, then." I looked him straight in the eye. "You have to decide how long you're going to give her before you go back there and bring her home?"

I hope you enjoyed this adventure with Ensley and Jack. Join them in their next exploit in Spirit Road.

About the Author

When Peggy isn't thinking up new ways to kill people, or how to blow something up she is growing orchids and blueberries, or taking her new 9mm to the range. She loves watching mysteries with her small but expanding zoo of two cats, two Spinoni. Outside lives a small flock of hungry Mallards complete with offspring, a gaggle of vexed Canadian Geese, the burgeoning covey of quail, and the hundreds of tiny toads who showed up this spring. The toads number has dwindled, but they are ever busy keeping the mosquito population at bay.

The dogs are clowns and the cats have learned to avoid the dog's large webbed feet. All four domestic animals are interested in the feathered crowd outside.

Her garden is an ongoing experiment. Gardeners in Idaho know that to grow anything other than sagebrush you have to make your own soil. That is the fun and the challenge of a thriving garden in the desert.

Also by Peggy Staggs

Ensley Markus Mysteries

House at Road's End

Deception Road

Spirit Road

Redemption Road

Crossed Roads

Justice Road (Coming soon!)

Laura Barlow Adventures

Cold Place in the Sun